Slow LOVE

to Gilbert

The Love Stories Of A Woman, Two Men, Their Dogs And Two Wolves

*with love
to some
weird
memories
Patrick*

Patrick Gossage

Slow Love
Copyright © 2021 by Patrick Gossage

All rights reserved. No part of this publication may be reproduced, distributed, or transmitted in any form or by any means, including photocopying, recording, or other electronic or mechanical methods, without the prior written permission of the author, except in the case of brief quotations embodied in critical reviews and certain other non-commercial uses permitted by copyright law.

Tellwell Talent
www.tellwell.ca

ISBN
978-0-2288-6679-4 (Paperback)
978-0-2288-6680-0 (eBook)

To my very patient wife Helga
for her love and caring for so many years

Table of Contents

Chapter One 1
Chapter Two 10
Chapter Three 18
Chapter Four.. 34
Chapter Five... 48
Chapter Six 60
Chapter Seven 70
Chapter Eight 89
Chapter Nine 105
Chapter Ten 115
Chapter Eleven... 131
Chapter Twelve 154
Chapter Thirteen.. 173
Chapter Fourteen 204

The Author 217

I love thee with a love I seemed to lose
With my lost saints. I love thee with the breath,
Smiles, tears, of all my life; and, if God choose,
I shall but love thee better after death.

Elizabeth Barrett Browning –
How do I love thee – Sonnet 43

Chapter One

Charles K. James is a typical successful business guy. A 55 year old widower, he is a typical successful business guy. He lives in a two-story substantial house in the suburbs and has an unusual dog Mabel who he dotes on. While he is attached to his hobby of nature painting and enjoys his weekends and holidays at his cottage on a northern rocky lake, he has slowly realized that his life has lacked real romance and lively love. Of course, he loves his 32-year-old daughter Sammy, but his marriage with his late wife was fairly routine and he has started to yearn for a new and lively love interest. And he now has a focus on an attractive younger woman and her dog who he has seen in the park where he walks Mabel.

Charles believed as an absolute fact that dog people are more nurturing and caring than non-dog people. His mom Peggy used to say that "Dog is God spelt backwards and, like God, is the only source of unconditional love." He believed that and now he had decided to try and get close to a real dog person, hopefully this attractive younger woman.

Such a fortuitous meeting was finally in the cards, and it began on a spring day in a woodlot in suburban Toronto. This nearby well-treed park where he now walks his dog becomes radiant with a blanket of trilliums in the early spring. The kind of pastoral beauty that melts hearts, particularly of dog walkers who wind up and down its myriad wide well-worn trails.

Charles is the owner of a successful PR firm. He is attractive, medium height and a bit overweight, with a strong nose, a thin face, lots of hair that's now salt and pepper but turning white, friendly brown eyes and a ready crinkly smile.

He was a relative newcomer to the woodlot with Mabel, his year-and-a-half old multi-coloured Australian sheepdog, who was bred to herd cattle. Her stubby tail, as he explained to all, was cropped to prevent the cattle from stepping on a bushy tail.

His wife had recently died of breast cancer very quickly after being diagnosed. During her short illness, Mabel was always a nearby caring and worried companion. Charles was trying manfully to keep house and dog happy for his beloved daughter, Sammy. Luckily, Sammy worked for a small marketing and public relations company in the suburbs and could come home at noon and walk Mabel while Charles was running his company in the city. Both she and he were sociable, as was the dog, and the dog soon became known by the neighbourhood dog walkers.

However, Charles soon learnt that strangers, or newcomers like him, often did not get to know the actual names of the veteran regulars. Like the unspoken 'no names' rule on the commuter train, it is difficult to get beyond hellos in the woods. Casual hellos and talking about dogs was okay if you weren't part of the regular gang, but asking for formal introductions or details beyond "Trixie's mom" was a bigger challenge.

And this was his issue with the lovely Hollie. Another dog walker had revealed her name. "Oh yes, that's Hollie, Joe's mom." Seeing her through the winter or passing her on the trail, he had admired and decided she could be the one. She was almost his height, blonde, all fresh and bright-eyed with full lips curled at the edges in a constant grin. This he had made out even if she was bundled up in her red parka. He knew her dog, a big chocolate brown lab named Joe. But that's as far as it had gone. This spring day, he was determined to see if he could get to know Joe's mom better. Just maybe she could be the solution to his romance strategy.

Now that the weather was warmer, he could see more of her. Her hair was showing now, and was long and very blonde, with a slight curl. Hollie had a strong chin, perky nose, long neck and large blue eyes. Without the red parka covering her up, he could appreciate that she had an athletic body and an almost perfect figure. That day she was in a form -fitting ribbed light blue V-necked sweater, tight-fitting jeans, and white runners. White cuffs turned up over the sweater's sleeves added a touch of class.

Charles thought of the first female dog owner he had fantasized about when he used to walk Mabel around his block first thing in the morning, rather than bringing her to the woodlot. She was a small redhead with a big toothy smile, thin hips and full breasts. Her dog was named Chester and she took an instant liking to Mabel. He introduced himself to her after meeting several times. But then one day as Charles watched her walk up her driveway towards a red pickup truck, he witnessed a very large and good looking young man embrace her. For some reason Charles was turned off.

Pre-work and weekend walks were the time to meet the dog crew in the woodlot. This sunny Sunday was no exception and 11:00 a.m. was a popular time for the long circuit.

That May morning Charles was feeling lonely as he scanned the beauty of the scene—the carpet of white and pink trilliums in the sun-dappled hardwood forest of beech, maple, and oak. As he often did, he was feeling sorry for himself with nobody with which to share the splendor of nature that he would photograph and then paint in his basement studio.

He had to admit his late wife did not share this love, which he had been dedicated to capturing in his unappreciated oil paintings. Luckily, his daughter shared his reverence, but then she was his daughter. She hung several of his works in her small apartment. At the moment, Sammy was the only woman in his life, but that was not the same as having a life partner, which he was almost ready to contemplate again.

He was hoping he would run into Joe—he and Mabel were already pals and maybe he'd actually meet his delicious owner and could at least work up a girlfriend situation of some sort.

Curiously enough, Hollie was having the same thoughts as she wound towards him on the wooded narrow lower path beside the stream. She had had a long-term live-in relationship with Bob, a big bruiser of a man who had been a turn on in bed but not much else. Recently, she had finally given him his walking papers after admitting to herself how little else they shared. She would explain the breakup to her friends with, "Joe never liked him, and showed it!"

With no children, she made an okay living doing illustrations for children's books—mostly cuddly animals of all sorts. Bunnies were her specialty. She did still like men, and she liked sex. But for now, she was unready to contemplate a new relationship that might exact too great a cost to her self-worth. She was a very self-aware 35-year-old.

Her dog Joe was a dark brown, large Labrador with a long full tail. He was a typical loving, easygoing and lolling about lab. "My only true boyfriend," she would say. She knew Mabel and had taken a good look at her manly owner over the winter and she too wondered if they'd actually meet that sunny day.

Just past the fallen log that had been sawn in two for the path, there they were, face to face, the dogs greeting each other with obscene sniffs and wagging. They were immediately jumping on each other in a doggie boxing match. After hellos, Charles and Hollie each waited for the other to start a conversation.

"They sure like each other," Charles offered first.

"They really do…" Hollie didn't know where to take this. Charles did. He'd been thinking about it for several weeks. That was a characteristic of this man—to be captivated by the image of a person he hadn't even really met. His good friend and number two at his firm, Ashleigh, teased him about this. "You always have to be in love with someone," she would say. And she was right. Even happily married, more or less, Charles would go to sleep dreaming of one of the "yummy mummies" he had barely met at the gym. As he would remind himself with the line from a song, that it is hard to be happy with your heart is on the run. Lately, his heart was fixated on Joe's owner.

"You know," he started hesitantly. Hollie moved closer, all ears. "It's ridiculous we don't even know each other's names and we've crossed paths a dozen or more rimes in the last months. I'm Charles and you are…?"

"Hollie. Pleased to put a name to a face."

"So am I. Aren't the woods spectacular today? I'm really inspired by the display of trilliums."

"They are amazing. I actually dug a few up and planted them in my tiny garden a few years ago. I know you're not supposed to…but a couple finally came up just now." She made a sweet girlish guilty-looking face.

"We'll forgive you," Charles said. "Do I detect a slight accent?"

"Yes, my parents are Dutch and came her when I was ten. So, English is my second language—but it never held me back. I did manage to graduate from the Ontario College of Art."

"So how old is Joe?" When in doubt, default to dog questions.

"He's two and a handful…takes a lot of care. But since I work at home, I can walk him several times a day."

"Wish I could walk Mabel as often. Luckily, my daughter Sammy takes her out most lunchtimes. We got her before my wife was sick and she was very much her dog, particularly when she was ill and Mabel kept extremely close to her. She knew what was happening. A very caring animal. Sammy loves her, she's a remaining connection with her late mom."

"Oh, I'm sorry—your wife passed away, then?"

"Yes, of cancer, a year ago." He felt perhaps he wasn't showing enough regret. He'd admitted to himself he was bad at death, even his own wife's.

She sensed that. "But you've survived?" Asked kindly.

"Yes, thanks. And Mabel has too. But she moped for a good month, looking for her, after my wife passed." By this time the dogs were jumping around the underbrush beside the path. He had an idea that would see the continuation of what seemed to have started that day. "I have a big yard and perhaps you'd like to bring Joe around for a play date some day?"

She responded—almost too warmly, she thought to herself. "I have a postage stamp yard in an apartment building. I'd love to—maybe next Saturday."

"Sure, let's meet here at the south woodlot entrance at eleven, we'll go for the long walk then to my house for a beer and doggie play. Sound good?"

"Okay. Until then." And with a wide grin on her face, she passed him and went off down the path in the other direction, Joe watching with interest. His dad had told him that a good way to judge a woman was to watch her walk away and judge her bearing. He watched Hollie walk away with a bit of a swing of her small round hips, straight, erect and proud. She passed the dad test.

The next Saturday was another stunning spring day with all the pungent smells of nature coming to full life in the mature hardwood forest. The paths had dried out and their carpet of dead leaves was almost crunchy underfoot. At the top of the south entry path at the end of the Mahogany Street cul-de-sac Charles waited patiently with Mabel on her long leather leash. Finally, an old Toyota Camry pulled up and out came a lovely slim leg with white running shoes followed by the full Hollie in fitted pedal pushers and a light blue cardigan over a white shirt—a trademark, Charles thought as he enjoyed her angling out of the car, then opening the back door and extracting the large bouncy Joe.

Great affectionate doggie hellos and Charles dared reach out to Hollie and pull her gently towards him for a perfunctory hug. She did not resist in the slightest.

Charles was pleased with himself—one minor physical barrier broken.

With the 'how are you's' over, they tripped down the narrow entry path and up the other side to where the main wide path began. An older couple with a tiny poodle as white as snow nodded hello as they passed. The two dogs paid no attention as they were off in the woods after a black squirrel.

"I don't believe it." Charles offered. "They are hunting together."

"I think they are having a full-on affair." Hollie answered impishly.

As Hollie's life story unfolded, it would be centered on finding and keeping love, appreciating the depth of love dogs had for her, she had for them, and they had for each other, and illustrating stories of animal love. Years later she would discover the love that the leaders of a wolf pack had for each other and for their pack, and would apply her talents to telling that story.

But this day she was watching Charles closely, deciding he was very attractive. Sort of ageless, she thought. She was very curious.

"I have no idea how old you are, Charles. Mind revealing yourself?" She tried to put it cleverly. Oh my God, she thought, I really am trying to impress him. What am I doing?

"Not at all." Charles answered. He was used to people underestimating his age. And quite proud of it. "I am 55."

It was a good reaction. The one he expected.

"No, you sure don't look it. Way to go—do you use some magic cream?"

"No, genetics, I suppose. My dad looked 50 at 65. But give it back—I know I'm not supposed to ask, but what's your age?"

"Not a day over 35—and unmarried and no kids. Might as well get it all out in the open." Yikes, Charles thought, she's only a few years older than my daughter.

A trio of local moms were approaching with a variety of dogs. Much sniffing and wagging as Mabel and Joe returned from the hunt to say hello. There was another Australian sheep dog and Charles exchanged herding banter with its tall disheveled owner in baggy pants. Hollie was certainly a standout among these ladies, well-coiffed and well turned out, Charles thought, that's her European background for sure. He had travelled quite widely in his youth in France and the Low Countries and was always impressed by the care their women took to look good in public. Not a known habit in the Canadian suburbs.

They parted from the group and continued down a steep hill, past some very tall old hardwoods with very tangled and gnarled roots—the subject of Charles's recent oil paintings—and towards the bottom of the narrow path by the stream where they _ had first broken the ice. They didn't talk much, enjoying the fresh air and listening to the "tap tap tap" of a woodpecker echoing from some distance. The leaves were just starting to come out and the sun still striped brightly through the trunks on the blanket of trilliums covering the ground. The dogs ran ahead, and Charles led Hollie in single file along the narrow path. They came to the sawed log.

"Hey this is where I found out who you were a week ago." Charles found himself saying. Unwittingly setting himself up for the answer he got.

"You mean this is some sort of anniversary? Isn't that pushing things a bit?" Doesn't miss a trick, Charles thought—I'm really starting to like her. He had to match her repartee.

"If you insist. Never know how things start." He meant it.

"You know the challenge with new relationships is about who makes the first move—especially when you are young, and we aren't!" She was not quite sure where this was going, but she continued.

"I have been out with lots of guys over the years and it was always they who made a move on me. I'm independent and rebuffed them more often than not. I'd like to choose who I build a relationship with. Do you understand?"

"Sort of. I was not very aggressive in my dating years for sure. So, we would have got on if you made the move on me." He remembered how he had pretty much fallen into his relationship with his first wife. It was sort of arranged. She was the daughter of family friends who had a nearby cottage; the right girl. They really did not become very passionate until after they were married, though he was not about to admit any of this to this obviously worldly younger woman.

"Well, all I can say is that I really got tired of always having to wait for the man to decide if this was going to go somewhere. Surely, I can have a say?"

"I agree on principle. But ideally it should grow on its own, don't you think? When the time is right, it should become obvious."

"I think you're right. As long as the woman has a real strong role in the decision."

"I can't disagree. But I just met you—so let's just be patient."

He was a bit confused by her seeming to talk about a scenario of them becoming that serious this soon. He would find out that simply that was just the way she was.

An hour later, after Hollie followed his smart silver Lexus in her old white Camry to his modest house five blocks away, they settled down with a beer each on his low deck overlooking a rather unkempt garden of sorts.

The dogs were sniffing around the yard and occasionally having a friendly boxing match.

The conversation started to get a bit serious, they both thought, sensing a need to feel each other out a bit on the subject of former partners, one dead and the other set aside. Hollie started it.

"So, Charles, was your late wife the love of your life? Were you devastated when she passed? Sorry to ask but these things do shape character. I think I need to know more about you before we get too far along—agree?"

"I suppose so." Charles hated to talk about his late wife Patricia. He felt very conflicted since the last years had seen them growing apart after their only daughter left home. "Well, Patricia and I had a wonderful daughter Sammy who kept us happy for a long time. But thirty-three years and what can I say? Her cancer was very hard for me to take. It was quite quick."

"Sorry, didn't mean to pry."

"No problem. I have to come to terms with my feelings. It will take time."

"I'm a bit in the same boat." Hollie felt the need to share her partner story and had to stretch it to make common ground. "Bob was a fairly ordinary good guy who was a friend of a guy I worked with. We went out and were physically attracted to each other and he moved into my condo—a bit prematurely, I now realize. I had not had many boyfriends. I'm fussy. Very fussy. But the hormones hit with Bob. In a year or so I knew it was too shallow and I had to get out. And I did. He was pissed. Convinced there was someone else. There wasn't—just my self-respect and Joe, of course. So, I have something to come to terms with too. Sorry, I probably told you more than you need to know."

"Well, Ms. Fussy, I'm flattered that you'd open up to this older guy."

"Age is only a number. And I sense there's more to you than there was to Bob. And you are creative—I saw your slightly evil-looking root paintings in the hall. Very original. I do illustrations for children's books."

"I'm impressed. I have only sold paintings for charity. And I couldn't do animals. Tried to sketch Mabel once, and it was a disaster."

"I'd be happy to do her portrait. Oh, and by the way I noticed there are chew marks on the legs of this furniture. Signs of an undisciplined puppy?"

"Yup. Mabel chewed and there are a lot of what we called 'Mabel marks' in this house. Did you have a non-chewing puppy?"

"Guess I was lucky. He just liked running around with my underwear. A proper canine fetishist. But he got over it!"

As they chatted on, building bridges of awareness as is so normal for men and women looking for a relationship, the two dogs had come on to the deck and were curled up squeezed on Mabel's big donut bed. Pals for sure.

Hollie suddenly felt a bit exposed. She had opened up too much and she had been a bit forward. God knows what this serious waspy guy thinks of me, she thought. He doesn't seem like a typical older man looking for a fling with a younger girl, but what do I know? But there is a mutual attraction, I think.

"I think I'd better break up the lover dogs." She said, moving over and leaning down to pat the dogs on the big bed. "I have a project to finish today."

"Really?" There was disappointment in Charles's voice. "Oh well, whatever, we'll meet in the woods, eh?"

"Yes, and let's do this next Saturday. I've enjoyed getting to know you a bit more." An understatement, she thought.

"The feeling is mutual." He got up and they walked through the house to the door. Hollie noted that it was in a bit of disarray.

"Clearly no woman lives here." She couldn't resist.

"The cleaning lady forces me to tidy up—she comes on Mondays. Lucky you."

They faced each other at the door. He looked into her clear blue eyes. But they were cool; no hint of affection. No kiss, he thought. They did hug each other very briefly. He opened the door and she and Joe got into her Toyota and he waved her away. Confused.

Chapter Three

The next Saturday followed a trying week at the office. A client wanted to do some serious downsizing and Charles's advice, which was not taken, was to be upfront about it right away and tell the public. Charles woke at 8:30 a.m. and thought about the day before. He remembered dreaming about Hollie being curled up beside him in bed. It upset him to think she had so soon invaded his dream life. In his experience, most dreams remained just that. Oh well, he thought—we'll see where today goes. If nowhere, nothing lost.

He had his shower, making sure to shave properly, with just a dab of expensive French aftershave cream. Frying up his Saturday treat of bacon and eggs, he pondered who this really attractive woman could be and whether he would continue the chase. What if he caught her? Mabel was in her usual morning breakfast pose—watching him intently and waiting for scraps.

He was now quite used to living alone, with no daily "reporting" of everything he did or even felt. And he was finally able to put his paintings up on the wall. Most of Patricia was gone, but there were lots of photos of his daughter at various ages, and sitting on the sideboard was one silver framed professional portrait of his late wife looking lovely but a bit severe.

He took Mabel downstairs and put her into the backyard then fed her. He sat down on the sofa and spread out the paper beside him. Mabel forced herself in behind him and put her head around on his lap. Big brown eyes looking into his.

"Hey young lady." Charles needed someone to talk to. "What is your affection-starved old master to do? I know you give me lots. But you like Hollie and Joe, don't you? That's a good start, eh? Should I let it get serious? You know it could." He was in the habit of admitting things to his dog, who grunted knowingly and then let out a loud post-breakfast belch.

He turned to the paper and tried to get his mind off Hollie. He then picked up the local paper, where a photo of a very fit handsome man with a group of teenagers caught his eye. It was a local judo club that was returning as champions from a tournament in Buffalo. The coach was a Bob Short. He wondered if it was Mollie's Bob. A good specimen of manhood.

"Is you ex Bob a judo coach?" He couldn't wait to find out and posed the question as soon as she joined him on the path at 11:05.

"As a matter of fact, he is. You saw his picture in the local rag?"

"Yeah—good looking dude, for sure."

"Can't fault him in the looks department, and he's dedicated to those kids and I found that appealing. He was built for speed…" He loved her double entendres. "Funny you should bring him up. He called out of the blue on Thursday. I'm at a bit of a loss and worried. He lost his job and wants to see me and pushed as to whether I was seeing anyone. Sorry, I said I was—aren't I?" She gave him a come-on look and continued, "Anyway he was upset, I could tell. He told me whoever it was had better treat me well. He was always jealous and protective—so be warned, Charles!" She gave 'warned' a nice ironic twist.

"Oh dear, I consider myself warned and assure you of only proper behavior from now on."

"Well, hope you don't take that too far. I like gentlemen, but a little fun, too."

"Well, I was thinking about dinner one evening—that could be fun."

"Sure, and it could be a proper date—no dogs. And you could pick me up and take me home—when did you last do that?"

"Oh, over 20 years ago." And in both their minds was the possible kiss at the doorstep.

"Well, I hope you haven't forgotten how to behave!" She said and laughed. He reached out and put his arm around her shoulder. Her head fit nicely in the hollow of his upper body. They both realized they were a good fit—that way at least.

It was a wonderful hour-long walk. They shared stories of their work and their families. Charles was relieved that Hollie loved her brother and her parents. Patricia's father and mother drank too much and fought a lot. He always felt it affected her ability to be open and loving. She could not wait to get away from them and they saw little of them after their marriage. Hollie's family, the Jansens, were a tight family for sure. Her father owned a successful cabinet making shop and her mother was a nurse. Hollie's brother, who was married and had produced a niece for Hollie, worked with his father. Hollie was interested in Charles's company James PR, as he described its 22 employees, nearly all women, many of them young and attractive, Charles admitted.

"Were you ever tempted by any of your young lovelies?" Hollie couldn't resist.

"At times, but my vice-president Ashley warned me not to fish off the company pier. So, I never did."

"Good boy."

"So, isn't your work a bit lonely?"

"Not as lonely as you'd think. I have a couple of authors I've done several books for, and you get to know them well. One, Jonathan Macintosh, is a Scottish guy I became good friends with before I met Bob. In fact, he was Bob's neighbor and introduced me to him. Would probably have been better off with him."

"So, what are you going to do about Bob?" He had visions of this big and obviously tough guy coming back and making trouble.

"I don't know…I have to convince him it is really over. I hope he isn't convinced he still loves me. He used to tell me he did often enough. But Joe never warmed to him—I should have taken that as a sign. Dogs know right?" Charles agreed and was relieved that Joe and Mabel loved each other at first sight, and that Mabel liked Hollie.

"Well, you know men and professions of love. Particularly if they want something."

"Don't be so cynical. He did have it pretty good living with me, the rent was cheap and I cooked. He was a window installer. Not a very fulfilling job."

"Will you see him?"

Slow Love

"Haven't decided." That ended that. They walked on in silence.

Both dogs suddenly put on a huge burst of speed as a black squirrel appeared in the distance crossing the path. They didn't even come close as he was up the nearest tree in a flash. They came galloping back for a treat from Hollie. Charles admitted that Mabel had never ever come close to catching a hated squirrel. Neither had Joe.

They did decide that the following Thursday would be date night and that Charles would pick her up at 7:00 p.m.

The day came and Charles put on his brown silk sports jacket and a light brown linen shirt open at the neck, good gray slacks and his best loafers. Then off across a wide avenue to the main street of their suburban town, north a few blocks to the second of two side-by-side 1950s apartments. He checked the address, and this was hers.

He was nervous and did not know what to anticipate from this very decisive vibrant woman who clearly had a mind of her own and was going to be hard to impress. And being Dutch she had that European edge and flavour that was very new to Charles, who had only known good vanilla establishment Canadian girls. Mabel was no help when he consulted her. Didn't even grunt. Charles was also used to weaker women who needed his help. Patricia fell into that category. The determined Hollie didn't. At least not yet, as he was soon to find out.

He buzzed her first-floor apartment from the slightly downscale lobby and a voice responded clearly, "Be right along." She wore a dark blue pencil skirt with matching low heels, that crisp white shirt, and a casual woolly jacket with a wide collar. Her hair was up in a full bun and she was discreetly made up. He thought she looked absolutely great.

They hugged formally and he took her to his car in the lot opposite the entrance. He was surprised to see an old black, rusty Ford 150 pickup two stalls down with large figure in the driver's seat. Hollie didn't notice.

She was anxious to tell him about the week's news of her meeting with Bob the ex. Charles thought it a bit odd to open his date evening on that subject, but so be it. He was a good listener.

"You wouldn't believe it. It's Monday at 6:45 in the morning the bell rings and it's Bob at the door. He looks tired and unshaven. He's going on and on about being fired and short of money. Believe it or not he is couch surfing with local pals but running out of places to stay.

"He was not pleased when I told him no way he was going to move back with me. He did a lot of 'Ah, come on's' and even grabbed me. I pushed him away.

"Then he moved on to what was obviously the real reason he had come. Seems his dad had given him a 1967 Centennial Canadian one-dollar gold coin and he could not find it. He's checked it out and it was worth over a thousand dollars. He was desperate to find it and thought he must have left it in the apartment."

* * * * *

At this point they had reached the restaurant in a strip mall. Charles was parking a short walk from the entrance.

"Let's continue the story when we sit down," he allowed.

He took her arm, ushered her in to the maître d' and the slim dark man took them to a table in a corner banquette. Charles led her on to the padded seat and he sat opposite on a well-padded armchair. A black-suited waiter appeared, and they ordered a bottle of Chardonnay.

"So, where was I? Oh yes, the missing coin. Well, insist as he might, I tried to convince him I had cleaned out the drawers he had used in the chest we shared, checked the closet and the desk in the living room and no traces of him were left in the flat. He wanted to search himself and got quite edgy with me when I refused. And he repeated his warning about whoever was taking me out. He asked who you were. I just said a nice man I had met walking the dog. He never liked the dog. 'That mutt!' he exclaimed. 'Lucky Joe, he still has you. I'm an outcast.' He was quite pathetic. He got up and made sure I knew that the treasured gold piece had better not be in the apartment. He left and slammed the door."

"Are you a bit frightened?" Charles to the rescue.

"A bit. To make me even more uneasy, I'm not sure if I got his key to the apartment back. He left in a big hurry. Hope he doesn't have it—I can't find my second key in any case. A very disorganized unreliable type. But he's mad at me, that's for sure."

"So, you just had one call from him and then he shows up at the door. Right?"

"Yes. I was not going to see him. I'd decided there was no point."

Suddenly Charles thought of the black pickup with the man in it. His heart raced.

"What kind of car does Bob drive?"

"An old Ford pickup—a disgusting truck."

"Jesus, Hollie. I think he was parked in front of your apartment when we left for the restaurant."

She paled. "Oh my God. If he has the keys, I bet he's searching my place for his bloody coin."

"We'd better go and see." Charles put on his saviour persona—one he had used courting the frail and moody Patricia.

"Do you mind? I sure don't want to face him alone, if he's there."

"Rescuing damsels in distress is a specialty of mine." He said this half-jokingly. Underneath he was worried about a string of what ifs. Like what if the guy was violent?

He persuaded the waiter to let him have the open wine, which he hid under his sports jacket. He paid for it, and off they went, both quietly apprehensive. Hollie knew Bob had a temper.

Sure enough, the light was on in the first floor apartment as they pulled around. And the Ford pickup was parked where Charles had seen it.

"He's in there—shit!" There was a slight tremble in Hollie's voice.

They walked down the hall and Hollie put her key in the door. She pushed it open.

"Bob, are you in there?" She shouted.

"Yeah, sorry, I had to see for myself if my coin was here. Let myself in. I still had a key."

They came into the living room and there he stood. Joe was laying on the couch growling with a low rumble, then left the room. Bob, all six feet of him, towered over them. Brush cut. Large square face. Jean jacket and old jeans and dirty high-top running shoes. Looking sheepish but unapologetic. The desk drawer was open, and he'd obviously been looking through it.

"Is this the new boyfriend?" he asked provocatively.

"He's a friend who is a man, not a boy." She retorted. "I'm pissed with you, Bob. How dare you come back in here without asking and rummage through my things. I told you there was nothing of yours here."

"Look sweetie, I had to be sure. It's the only thing of value I had and I'm broke. And I'm sure as hell not getting any sympathy from you after a year of looking after you. And by the way, that mutt of yours damn near bit me when I let myself in."

"Don't 'sweetie' me, Bob. And Joe was protecting me. Hey, I looked after you and don't owe you anything. Now please leave and don't come back again—ever."

"Is your wealthy friend going to make me?"

Charles was on the spot now. A much bigger Judo trainer was daring him to do the manly thing and show him out forcefully if necessary. Charles hadn't hit anyone since he punched a tough kid who had been bullying him in Grade 5 and made his nose bleed.

"Look, Bob. You know perfectly well I can't force you to leave and would be foolish to try. Why don't you just leave quietly and apologize to Hollie for being here in the first place. And give her back her key."

"You're a pussy. I'd love to flatten you—it would be too easy." Bob was blistering. Hollie looked terrified.

"Please, Bob. Don't spoil what we had with this. I hate it when you lose control. Get a hold of yourself. Please!" She pleaded.

This stopped him and he suddenly looked like a kid whose mother had scolded him.

"Okay, here's your goddamned key. But your new buddy better look out. I want you back and I intend to get you back. I'm out of here." He threw the key at her feet and stormed out. Hollie threw herself into Charles's arms, shaking.

Charles knew he hadn't done anything to quiet the confrontation. It had been her. But at least he was there.

"Thank God I was not alone with him." She pulled him tight against her firm breasts. "Sorry you were almost set up for a bruising."

"Hey, I was pretty useless. You got to him. Not me."

"Yes, but I had the courage to, with you as my backup."

"Well, let's have the wine and reconsider the evening. It's all a bit too much."

"You said it. Okay, I'll get glasses. Joe must have gone to the bedroom. I'll fetch him."

She went out leaving Charles to reconnoiter her living space. It was modest but tasteful. Modern Swedish/Ikea style, three-seat couch and matching armchair. A nicely upholstered older wing chair and in an L-shaped part off the main room a teak dining room set with five chairs.

There was a nice classic six-drawer antique writing desk with a couple of framed photos on it—one obviously of her family in younger years and another colour blown-up snap of her hugging Joe the dog. Very homey. The end of the room had large windows with quality chintz curtains drawn and he could see in the dining alcove a sliding door which must open out to a tiny garden. The kitchen was attached and obviously a bedroom came off the main hallway. She must have her studio in there, he thought.

Joe came in, with much wagging and nuzzling. He smelt his pal Mabel on Charles's clothes. Hollie got glasses from the kitchen and returned. Charles retrieved the bottle from the desk where he had put it and poured.

"Here's to Bob-free days." They clinked on it, Charles stretching over from the wing chair opposite Hollie on the couch.

"Think it's a bit of wishful thinking to believe I've seen the last of him." Hollie said sadly. "Sorry to get you involved."

"No problem. But I hope I don't meet him in a dark alley."

"Never know with Bob."

"Was he ever violent with you?"

"No. More threatening if he thought I was showing interest in someone else. And I think he knew I was interested in you."

"Oh, you are then. Nice to know when I may have to take on your brute of an ex to win you."

"Unlikely. Hey are you hungry? I could make you grilled cheese and pickles. Not much of a date dinner. But might as well stay here and drink the good wine. And I have another bottle if we need it." She was mildly flirting, curled up on the couch with her dog beside her, showing some leg.

"Okay, if you insist. But I do want to see your studio."

"Sure. Follow me." They went out into the hall and into a large bedroom that also had big windows on the same side as the dining room, looking into a grassy area with a small tree. That is where she had her large easel set up with her drawing equipment on a big side table. Next to it was a small desk with laptop. There were sketches of some wonderful cozy looking red squirrels with bright eyes and big bushy tails on a large sheet on the easel.

"This is for a book about Chatty the red squirrel." She explained.

"My working drawings to show the author. A nice young guy called Warren Jones."

"They're wonderful, Hollie." He meant it.

"Yeah. I like them. I haven't done many squirrels before. But they are turning out all right."

She turned out the lights and they went back to the living room. He stayed with the dog and she busied herself making the sandwiches.

They seemed to appear in no time—nicely plated on flowered china on the dining room table. He brought the wine over and they sat down opposite each other. The sandwiches were good, as were the dill pickles.

"Like all single people I consider myself a grilled cheese connoisseur," he allowed. "These are as good as I make and that's saying something. I add a bit of mustard and I can see you do, too."

"Of course. Thank you, Monsieur."

They finished the restaurant bottle and Hollie opened another—Pinot Grigio this time. They were both warmed, the trials of the early evening forgotten.

They squeezed together side by side on the sofa, Joe pushing Hollie in at the end, his big brown head on her lap.

"I have competition." Charles admitted.

"For what? To see who is more affectionate? Think you could win in that department?" It was her not unexpected invitation.

Charles took it and put his arms around her and pulled her towards him and kissed her gently. She responded gently.

"Well, that's a start—or is it?"

"Since I really haven't properly kissed anyone for a few years, you can be the judge." They kissed again more passionately. She drew away.

"That was nice." She was indecisive, not sure how far she should let this go. She knew herself well enough that if they started to engage with their tongues, which she really liked, she would get turned on and that would be that.

He understood her reticence. "Look, maybe for tonight we should stop there. Life is complicated and we're both grownups with a bit of a past. I know we want to be sure. Life is serious at my age."

"Oh dear. I agree and this Bob thing must be settled. Plus, I do want to know you better. I don't have a lot of kicks at the can left. But you are a good kisser."

"Well, thanks. I think there is more to me. Let's do some things together. Like going to the art gallery, and even a movie. Maybe we share tastes. That would be nice."

"It sure would be, after Bob. He liked monster truck rodeos."

"Okay it's a deal—it will be getting to know each other for a while. Then maybe we can take up where we left off tonight."

"I look forward to that, assuming we still like each other." She meant it. She did miss good sex.

"And let's leave love out of it unless it just happens. Okay?"

"I agree—vastly overrated—and I heard enough of it from Bob."

Chapter Four

The following Saturday instead of walking their dogs they travelled south into the city to the Art Gallery of Ontario, which was having an exhibition of the late Canadian figurative artist Alex Colville—a favorite of Charles. He was eager to see how Hollie would react to some of his difficult and highly realistic symbolism. Particularly his paintings featuring lethal-looking handguns, including one with a large automatic pistol on a table and the bare torso of the artist's back as he gazes out at the ocean, and another with a nude woman with a revolver. And the iconic *Horse and Train*, in which a horse gallops along the track towards the distant headlight of an approaching train. Lots to talk about, Charles thought.

They found a place to park on a side street and crossed to the wide modern entrance. Charles had a membership and bought a ticket to the special show for Hollie. Their time for entrance was a half-hour away, so they went to the bright gift shop and he bought the catalogue for an appreciative Hollie. They sat together on a bench near the entrance to the show and Hollie leafed through the large colour catalogue.

"Hey!" she exclaimed. "there's a fascinating bit here in the intro by the show's curator in which he tells about meeting a Chinese artist years ago who was very familiar with Colville's work—in particular the *Horse and Train*—this one." She leafed through the plates and found it. "Wow," she exclaimed. "This is really strong. Anyway, he says a Chinese artist said how it inspired his radical friends who saw echoes of this image in the lone man standing up to the tanks in Tiananmen Square."

By this time their slot was open. In they went and quickly found the real thing. Hollie was transfixed. Charles could not have been more pleased. They came to *Pacific*—the man's back with the gun on the table.

"I always found this quite ominous." Charles said.

"I think it's a bit evil and maybe shows a side of Colville that's a bit dark—despite all the other clean, fresh nudes, kids, and ordinary people in seemingly ordinary situations. I think everyone has a dark side."

"Haven't found yours yet." Charles said teasingly.

"Wait for it." She retorted.

Hollie loved all the animals in the exhibition—dogs, horses, even a coyote. All done with loving detail.

After an hour and a half, they had taken in the nearly 100 amazing paintings. They both felt full.

"What a great banquet of such strong memorable images!" Hollie exclaimed as they left the building.

"Couldn't agree more—so pleased you liked my favorite artist. Wish I could paint like him. But then he takes weeks to do one painting. It's his life. I just splash away."

"But I think anyone who does graphic art has a special appreciation for excellence in another's work. You know what it takes."

She was right on, Charles thought. He could remember every brush stroke on every painting he had ever done. He shared this with her and she agreed. Each animal she drew and finely coloured was physical work she could recall in detail—right down to the whiskers done with a tiny brush with just one bristle in it. This discussion and the whole day proved to him that they could share a lot in life.

Oh dear, he thought. This is such a mature way of becoming attached to a woman. Not at all like the instant "love" I felt for sad Patricia. To think of a canoe analogy, the wind is at our backs.

He confessed as much to Mabel that evening before going to bed.

She answered with a very knowing little yelp—a sound she did not make very often. Charles took it for approval.

Their next date brought their day of decision even closer. It was to be a movie on a weeknight. It was again one of Charles's favorites: a revival of the wonderful romantic comedy *Notting Hill* with Hugh Grant and Julia Roberts, on whom Charles had harboured a major crush for years. Hollie admitted she felt the same about Grant. It was perfect for an exploratory date. Things happen in dark cinemas, and both wondered if they would that night.

It did, right at the great moment when Roberts comes into Grant's bookshop and delivers the iconic line about being a girl facing a boy, asking him to love her. This leaves Grant's character totally perplexed, but sets up the dramatic ending in which they have a passionate embrace at her departing press conference.

Charles felt Hollie's hand taking hold of his hand—very tightly—as the line was spoken, and she brought it to her lips and kissed it fondly. He was so moved he did not know how to react to this, or to what she did next with his hand. She was about to make the first move. She put his hand on her breast and cupped it tightly over its firm roundness. Just for a moment, then she returned it. Charles took a deep breath, wondering if he was dreaming. This adorable woman wanted him and was making it plain.

They continued to feel each other out (verbally at least) on Saturday dog walks. It was clear in these walks that at least the two dogs were totally devoted to each other. Much nuzzling and kissing when they met, then Joe would be the leader and off they would go into the woods for five minutes at a time and back they would gallop, Joe still in the lead.

The two-legged friends had informal dates. One at the local Chinese-run rather basic fish and chips eatery in a mall, and another at a small place on the main street with allegedly the best hamburgers in town. No more provocative clinches, just close hugs and light kissing on the lips. Both were wondering when one would suggest a date that at least had the potential of leading to something more. Hollie realized she was still somewhat wounded from her unsuccessful year with bad Bob, and reticent to go beyond what she thought was an obvious invitation in the cinema.

She confided this to Joe one evening when he'd placed his large brown head firmly on her lap and was looking up at her with his huge brown eyes.

"Yeah, I know pal. You don't want to share me with another guy. I have to be all yours, right? Well, I'm not sure you'll have to. Not now at any rate. But guess what?

There is good chemistry, and that means a lot to me. We'll see. Don't worry. I know you like him and his cute Mabel." At the sound of his friend's name, he perked up briefly and yawned.

Charles pondered the issue of going further than he should and was as indecisive as Hollie. He knew that mature people who finally date again after trauma or hurt from previous relationships are not easily persuaded to rush into something else that might involve real new commitment. This was slow love indeed and not easy for either despite physical attraction. And some yearning on Hollie's part as she realized she really liked this older man.

Being an organized and disciplined Dutch girl, she decided to do a check list of pros and cons and decide whether he was indeed the right one. So, she got some squared paper out of her desk drawer and started writing pros and cons about this potential mate. Charles had once reminded her of the old line from a Pat Boone song about why making sure a date would make a good mate, so she would do just that.

She listed five personal characteristics, with space for pro and con checkmarks. She felt awful about it but the first was personal hygiene—this was a definite pro—Charles always was very clean and smelled nice. She could not go out with anyone that didn't. Next was polite and manners. Another pro—Charles held doors and walked on the correct side. Next was good listener. Not a complete pro so she put a dash for neutral. He did interrupt on occasion, as most men do. Finally, she wrote down calm and collected? She had known men with a temper and Charles appeared not to have one. So that was a pro. First run netted four out of five. Not bad. And of course, the dogs got on so well—not on her list but a plus for sure.

Now for the tricky stuff. Physically attractive? A pro. Could be good in bed? She did not know what to put. He was a good kisser, but since she considered herself accomplished in that regard, she had to hope if he wasn't, she could bring him along. So, she put a dash. Then a few practical worries, like would he help with housework? Pro—he had rushed to clean up the one time they had a meal at her house. By the look of his kitchen, he knew how to cook, too. Did he talk down to me? No, he took my opinions seriously—pro. Did they share the same interests? Certainly, in film, art and a whole lot of other things, including politics, which they had discussed on their walks. Both were left wing; thank goodness, she had thought. All good—pro. Finally, was he athletic? She was; she worked out and hated fat, slothful people. He had talked about how much he loved paddling his canoe at his cottage. And under questioning had admitted he had a stationary bike he used at home. He went to the gym occasionally. She had to give him a pro for trying even if he needs to lose weight. I can see to that, she thought. So again, that's four out of five. Nine out of ten total, she thought. Guess I'm for it. And I don't mind making the first move.

"I'm going to do it!" She told Joe who was spread out in front of her. He looked up at her, puzzled, then stretched right out with a loud groan.

And she did. It was classic. The next Saturday they got into some heavy exchanges on relationships and their mutual worries. She had admitted that she had gone out with good looking guys who were not very bright, but she was physically attracted to. Charles admitted that he'd played it very safe and stayed within his social circle when it came to dating. So, he ended up with Patricia, the attractive daughter of a neighbour at the cottage, who had quit university and worked as a receptionist in an upscale doctor's office. "I guess I went out with girls who were unsure of themselves and needed a strong man, which I thought of myself as being. Girls who weren't like you, for sure," he had found himself saying.

She knew they were getting closer and invited him to her house. She would make dinner. He would bring wine. This might be it.

Buzz buzz on the following Wednesday and she let him in and greeted him at her door in a low-cut long-sleeved silk shirt that exposed her perky breasts just enough, along with tight white pants and low slippers. She threw her arms around him and said enticingly "Welcome to my lair." Joe, the brown lab, was on him as soon as she let go with his own affectionate greeting. Charles felt a glow all over his body.

"That's the kind of greeting I needed," he admitted.

In the living room he could see she had set a table with fine linen napkins, place settings, candles, and crystal wine glasses.

"Expecting someone important?" he asked.

"No, just you." He asked for it.

"Well, here I am and here is the lubricant for the evening." And he gave her the bag with two good bottles of New Zealand Chardonnay. She took them to the kitchen. She was surprised at what he asked provocatively when she returned:

"Do you mind coming beside me on the sofa and giving me a real kiss?" He had decided on the drive to her house that he indeed liked her enough to take another step. A real kiss it was to be. For once he would make a move—a big deal for him.

As their tongues engaged and they kissed as deeply as either had ever before, they both knew this might indeed be the evening they got to another level. Or the first evening of what might be the rest of their relationship.

That was just what Hollie asked him when they finally sat still beside each other. Both tingling.

"Do you think this is the first evening of the rest of our relationship?"

"I was thinking maybe." He was not pleased by pulling his punches this way. She did not. Hoping.

"Well, I think it should be. We are in sync, eh? And as I said before, you are a good kisser," she added provocatively.

"Well, thanks. So are you."

"Gotta get the meal on the table…" And off she padded as he watched her wonderful behind swing out past the dining room.

The meal was a wonderful—breaded veal with roast potatoes and cauliflower with a white cheese sauce. Wine flowed and the conversation was easy. They talked about the young prime minister who was making some early gaffes and Hollie admitted that since he was good looking, well-built, and very athletic she would forgive him some political growing pains. Charles wanted to know more about her parents and found out that her dad had been the mayor of a town liberated in the second war by Canadians and later decided to emigrate and look up the colonel who had led the battle group into his town, which had succeeded. He lived in Toronto where they first settled. He was a businessman and had helped her father get started in his cabinet making business.

"We really had such love for Canadians." She admitted warmly.

They continued to exchange other life stories including Charles's tales of his dad and his love for the north country, building their cabin on a lake in Muskoka, his happy childhood puttering around boats, and his cedar strip canoe he got when he was 18 and still enjoyed.

Charles found out how Hollie got her name—from the word holiday. It seems since her dad had always planned on coming to Canada and saw that as a kind of holiday when they would finally achieve their dream, he wanted a happy English name, and he could not think of a better one. Their new life would be a holiday.

Hollie had a flashback as he went on about cottage life, a life she told him she had no idea about, although the Jansens had camped when she and her brother were young. The flashback had Bob sitting where Charles was as he had for a year at many dinners. The conversation often was about how unhappy he was in his boring job installing new windows in rich people's houses. But at least on many nights Hollie knew she was assured of good hard-core sex after the dishes were done. She looked at Charles relishing his meal and cottage memories and wondered how he would shape up—nice and sensitive as he was.

* * * * *

Meanwhile further south towards the big city in a messy old low-rise apartment, Bob was telling his oldest friend from high school days, Marco Messana, about his lost love and the creep she was dating.

"He's too good to be true. There must be something wrong with him. Would I love to get something on him and confront her with it. Mr. Slick, and he has money too. Drives a Lexus."

"So, what can I do to help?" Marco was worried about his pal, who had been occupying his sofa for three weeks while he tried to get a job. Obviously, he was deeply wounded by being dismissed by his girlfriend. Marco's family was Sicilian and he could sense revenge in the air.

"I just thought of something," Bob's face lit up. "You're a cop. Maybe Mr. Slick has a record. Would that be hard to find out?"

"Not something I'd do for just anyone. But it would be fun if he did." He had happy visions of his friend confronting his ex with much glee. "Okay, I'll see what I find."

* * * * *

Back at the dinner table with her new untested potential partner, Hollie realized both were nervous to see how the evening would end and who would make the first real move.

Finally, as is often the case, it just happened. Dinner ended, they both cleared up, put the dishwasher on, took a breath and embraced. Charles dared put his hand on her hard little bum and pulled her against him as they passionately kissed.

"I think we are for it." She whispered in his ear. "Come with me."

She led him into her bedroom and disappeared into the adjoining bathroom which had a door from the hall and one from the bedroom. She emerged in the flimsiest of shorty nighties. Charles took off his jacket and she unbuttoned his shirt, standing back to survey his slightly enlarged stomach but otherwise trim torso.

"Not bad, but if we get together you are going to lose weight." She sat him on the edge of the bed and helped him off with his shoes, socks and pants. She turned down the sheets, hopped into the bed and said, "Well, come on old guy. I'm ready. Hope you are."

He was. It was good. Not ferocious. Hollie did guide him to please her the way she liked. Something new and not natural to him. But he lasted and she was happy. He was over the moon. There wasn't much to say. It seemed like a beginning.

They decided to go to sleep in each other's arms and Charles would sneak out to rescue Mabel when Hollie was asleep. When he did so at 1:30 a.m., he was a happy man.

Slow Love

Charles called her in the morning on his cell from the train. Neither really knew what to say. Charles had an idea: why not come to his place the following Friday and he would cook? She liked the idea. He asked how the squirrels were going. She yawned and told him she now had the text and had to make them into real characters that did things following the plot. A lot of work.

"And something nice happened to me last night." She said coyly. "It did tire me out a bit. I'm going to the gym and wake up." She talked softly.

"Me too. I'm a bit wacked." He admitted having had only a few hours of sleep and was up early to walk Mabel. "Anyhow, maybe we need a bit more practice." He caught her with the obvious comment.

"Yes, I was thinking the same thing. Anyhow, talk soon." And they ended the conversation. Slow love seemed to be speeding up. They both considered—were they ready? Were there bumps to come?

Charles talked to Mabel that evening. He was honest:

"Don't know. This is all going too well. She is too wonderful. There must be some bumps in this road. She is very young for me." Mabel let out a long sigh and farted.

"Thanks for your understanding, Mabel!" He scratched her behind the ear.

Indeed, there were, and it was the unfinished Bob business which would cause problems in this smooth if extended run up to love.

Bob was determined to make problems for his ex's new relationship. As it turned out, Marco was able to phone Bob at his own place the following Thursday and announce enthusiastically that indeed Charles had a record of possession of marijuana from almost 35 years ago. Bob let out a loud yip when Marco told him.

"That's too amazing! So not the pure great guy he makes out to be, I'm sure. Wait until I tell Hollie. That's so damn good—thanks Marco. You're the best."

He decided to drive to her house and confront her the same day. He buzzed her just after five and after saying she didn't want to see him, when he said he had something really important to tell her, she let him in.

"So, what is so important?" she asked as he settled into the wing chair.

"Just a little thing I found out about your Mr. Wonderful. Seems he has a criminal record of possession of marijuana—I assume for dealing. He must have had a lot. Seems he got away with a large fine and community service. But he has a record. Told you he was not what he makes out to be. What do you think now?"

Hollie was taken aback, but not at a loss for words. "Well, I'm sure he will have some sort of explanation. I know him well enough to know he's not a criminal if that's what you're hoping—obviously."

"That's not the point. I just do not want you to get hurt. He didn't tell you, eh?"

"No. So what? It happened so long ago. Thanks for your concern." She said sarcastically. "But I know all you want to do is derail whatever good may be happening to me and someone else."

"Damn it, I still want to be with you. We had it good. I can't stand you being with this guy."

"Sorry. It's my life and we're over. So over. I cannot stand your jealousy. Never could. Now if you don't have anything else to reveal, I'd like you to go."

Bob felt crushed. He looked around at the flat he had lived in for a year and at the adorable woman he had surely loved. It was all too much. He felt himself losing it. He put his head in his hands and sniffled loudly.

"Come on Bob. You're a good looking guy. You'll find another woman. One who can love you. I'm sorry it didn't work out with us."

He sniveled. "I so need you now. I've got nothing. Just my truck and a suitcase with all my stuff and I'm couch surfing with my pal Marco."

She was not moved. "Well, shit happens to us all. But I can't help you."

He got up and stumbled out.

* * * * *

The next day Charles left work early to go home, walk the dog and prepare his specialty: steaks on the BBQ, oven-roasted potatoes with herbs, and green beans. Simple but good, he thought.

He set the table with his best white china and candles in their silver holders and put out real wedding present silver from Birks and white formal napkins. He opened two good bottles of a small Chateau Bordeaux to breathe and set to work.

He had to admit that he was worrying about their difference in age. It became more of an issue after a long conversation with his daughter Sammy. He admitted to her that "this Hollie thing," as she called it, was becoming serious. She right away demanded to know how old she was.

"Dad, are you crazy?" She had exclaimed with a lot of emphasis in her sharp voice. "She could be your daughter. And she doesn't sound like a possible trophy wife, but is she?"

He had told her she was anything but a babe—but was very attractive.

He had tried to soothe her. "She reminds me of you. She's very fit—not an ounce of fat on her."

"That's nice, but I don't need a sister who is married to my dad." She did have a tongue like her late mom, he thought.

So, this was what was on his worried brain as he parboiled the potatoes and chopped the beans.

Right at six-thirty the doorbell rang, Mabel barked, and he opened the door to Hollie in a blue mini skirt, hair tied into a ponytail, a revealing off-the-shoulder striped blue blouse, and Joe the dog. The dogs dove at each other and Charles hugged Hollie.

She looked through to the dining room.

"Nice setup. Looks like you got out the wedding china and silverware." She was feeling a bit wicked.

"How did you know?"

"Singles don't get those kinds of gifts." It crossed her mind that if it came to that with Charles, she'd likely have to settle for goodies from his marriage.

He got her a glass of wine and they sat opposite each other in his well-upholstered armchairs while the dogs wrestled on the fine large oriental rug. Hollie took in the room, which was much more luxuriously furnished than hers. The large sofa with obviously down-filled pillows and smaller designer ones thrown decorously in the corners. A large mahogany coffee table with double drawers with brass handles.

She was one to cut to the chase if she had something on her mind. And she did.

"So, dear Charles. My excellent ex got a cop friend of his to see if you have a criminal record. And as you know, you do. I was pissed with Bob with trying to make trouble for us. He only succeeded insofar as I was surprised. I thought you were the straightest of guys."

Charles was surprised and angry. "That jerk," was his perhaps too quick response. "I knew he was out to get me, so he digs up a mistake I made thirty-five years ago. I hope you don't think I was a dealer because I wasn't—I happened to be taking a bag of pot home for safety because our dealer, our secretary, thought the cops were after her. I was caught on a speeding stop and searched. I got a fine and had to do community service for a month which turned out well since I helped at a social service agency and eventually went on their board. I had the conviction removed. Some drug lord, eh?"

"Okay. You don't have to be so defensive. I was pissed with Bob too. Let's leave it. Wow, I've never seen you angry."

"It takes a lot. And jealousy can be so destructive. You aren't upset, are you?" he was genuinely concerned that somehow Bob had scored a victory against him, however small.

She felt his concern. "Don't worry I'm not scoring one for Bob. What he did was wrong. And finding out you're not perfect suits me!" She had the last word.

He went to the back deck to cook the New York steaks, leaving her alone with the dogs to ponder a future with this guy for the first time after the drug revelation. She realized he was a lot older with a lot more history. Including a grown daughter. How would this play out in a more permanent scene if it were to come to that? Would she have to give up independent living and move into this rather upscale place which was not really to her more basic taste? And what about their parents? She knew that his elderly mother Peggy was alive and living in a luxurious old people's residence. Her parents were both living in the modest family home in the modest district of East York. Her very tough, practical mom would be suspicious of this older waspy guy. And she'd ask about her having a kid. Would he want a baby at his age? Her dad would just say what he always did: "Whatever makes you happy, darling." In Dutch, of course.

But he was working his way into her consciousness and that kind of connection of two souls was starting to operate. It scared her a bit –it was new. He certainly accepted her more leading role in the development of their relationship.

Charles was furiously rushing between the BBQ and kitchen trying to time the meal. The potatoes were done and in the oven in a serving dish. Beans almost. And the steak just right. He had found out she liked her streak medium rare and one of the two would be for sure. Plates warming in the oven. *Three minutes*, he said to himself, slicing into the steaks. Indeed, the one on the front of the burner was rare, and the one in the middle was medium rare. Perfect. He flipped them on to a platter and marched them formally into the dining room with a loud and formal "dinner is served."

"Haven't you forgotten the veggies?" she asked ironically.

He rushed to get the potatoes out of the oven and the beans off the stove and on to another platter.

"The rest of the dinner is served!" He announced. She laughed.

The dinner went well. She downed the steak enthusiastically. Loved the potatoes. They talked about their very different parents. Turned out his were pretty establishment. His late dad had been a corporate lawyer and his mom a homemaker. Peggy had given up their big downtown house and moved into a luxurious retirement home two years ago. She only had a high school education. But she had been a beauty. Now over 80, Peggy was missing her family to which she had dedicated her life. Especially since her only other child, a daughter, had died of a rare brain disease at age ten and she had never really recovered from the loss. She still doted on Charles, he admitted, and he called her every day.

Some of this rambling description of his family gave Hollie pause. What if Peggy didn't like her? On the other hand, maybe she would be taken in as the lost daughter?

The James family history took them to dessert. Charles produced a store-bought apple crumble with whipped cream from a pressure can, for which he apologized. She accepted graciously.

Now, as they sat at the table holding hands, the time seemed right to address the big question: where was this going?

Hollie opened it up.

"Dear Charles, we've now been seeing each other, as they say, for almost two months. We shared a bed. And kissed madly. Done a bunch of things and the dogs are in love. Are we? And if so, what do we do? Is this a slam dunk?"

"You have nailed it—that's the question. And I'm not into gushing admissions of love. I thought we'd discussed that."

"Okay, okay, I agree." She felt a bit foolish. He was trying to be sensible, obviously, and she was ready for that given her pre-dinner thoughts.

"I've been thinking about our age difference, and I bet you have. And…" he continued, reading her mind, "there is the question of whether you'll want a family if we married. That's a big one."

"Sure is, and I don't know what to say. Have to say I do feel a bit incomplete. Most of my friends have kids. It does occupy my mind occasionally."

"How diplomatic. I have to say I'm not sure about having another family. I work with a guy who remarried at 60 and has a toddler. He is surely proud of being able to make one, but a bit overwhelmed. And not much help to his younger wife. Also gets a lot of teasing from his friends."

That's where the serious part of the evening ended. Charles had been an inveterate DJ at college in the later seventies and early eighties and he asked Hollie if she'd mind taking a bit of a musical voyage to his youth. She did not and he put on a collection of Kenny Rogers' greatest hits—the first cut being the very romantic "Lady." As the strings swelled, she got up, pulled him up from Mabel. Draped her arms around him and started dancing. It worked for both.

Fred Astaire and Ginger Rogers they were not, but it was cheek-to-cheek with a few Astaire flourishes that Charles knew. They ended up deep kissing as other less romancing cuts followed. Then it was, do we go to bed? The bed he shared for so many years with his late wife, Hollie thought. Curiously, he was thinking the same thing and starting to realize the downside of his old life as he was facing a new relationship. He was the first open the subject of lovemaking, and quite cleverly, he thought.

"I wonder if we should do it tonight. Not that I don't want to. But I don't think either of us want to put sex over being sensible. *Sex and Sensibility*, not a bad book title, eh?"

Luckily, they could laugh over the issue standing in the way of their carrying their affair to its logical conclusion.

"You are funny." She admitted with a grin. "Our minds sure work the same way. I think I can do without good sex for another few days. But let's not overthink this. Please?"

"Okay, but love is not simple. It's a long and winding and bumpy road. Question is, should we stay on it?"

"Well, we have to decide. I really like you and can't find much wrong with you or us—despite your druggy past!"

"Oh, you've done one of your lists?" He knew she was an inveterate list maker, having spied the neat prep list for the dinner she made for him on her kitchen counter. He was not.

"As a matter of fact, I did and didn't detect any major 'bumps' as you put it. Though I've thought of a few since. Like your daughter and what she thinks."

"You are so good at foreseeing things. Yes, can't say she's thrilled about me marrying someone just a few years older than her."

"Okay. But I'm so mature for thirty-five, don't you think?"

"What can I say? Yes, you are in many ways." He was tempted to say *for sure in the bedroom*. But stopped short of going there. She knew.

"I know what you're thinking: that I'm very mature in matters of lovemaking. And yes, I am. Lucky for you at this point!"

"Enough or we'll be between my sheets."

"You know I've thought I'd reconnect with Warren the squirrel guy. He's my age and I think I should look into him." Charles shuddered. But they got off a happy deep kiss he walked her and Joe to her car at the curb.

Slow Love

"See you soon." He said without a lot of energy.

"We'll see," she said opening her window. And he detected a tone of apprehension in her voice as if she wasn't quite sure when or if they'd restart their slow love.

Chapter Six

He told Mabel what had happened and that she might not see Joe regularly again. She did look sad. Who knows what dogs understand? Although he did notice her being a bit more mopey than usual for a few weeks when they did not see Hollie and Joe in the woodlot.

This unforeseen failure to make a real connection with a very different woman that he really wanted forced Charles into a bout of self-reflection about his life.

He was so used to easy success. He did well at school and at university. He found a good job in marketing at a big consumer goods company right out of college. That was when he was busted for possession. But it was not made public and didn't hurt his career. Later, he successfully applied to have his record wiped. After two years he was doing well and decided to form his own PR company. His dad underwrote his bank line of credit and he started with one employee, a mousy but effective girl who did the grunt work on early small clients. He made the correct marriage with Patricia who soon gave him an adorable daughter. It was not a deep crazy love but a sensible marriage. But it suited him. It was an easy scene, and he was deep into getting started at his firm and she was not involved.

Then a friend of his who worked at one of the big banks recommended him to help with their PR and he got the assignment. Again, relatively easy success. Soon he was running their annual meeting and later was writing speeches for the CEO. He had to admit to himself that it was his easy charm as much as his talent that often won the day.

Clients liked working with him. And when he hired the lovely tall blonde Ashleigh, they really liked working with her. They were a great team and soon had an airline client that flew them around to run promotional events they had dreamed up. At a staff retreat for their marketing department they even dazzled the group with a loud karaoke version of "You're so Vain"!

For outside work he had volunteered to do communications work at same downtown social service agency where he had done community work after his drug bust. He was soon put on the Board, and he helped them get some press for their work with young people. He became involved with their youth-at-risk program, one of the few in the very poor social housing district that helped young people who had little hope and were apt to get into guns and gangs. Their youth worker Steve, a tough island guy, knew that Charles painted and arranged for a showing of his Northwoods paintings. The showing was a success, with friends and clients buying canvases for their cottages. Charles was very pleased, as the money raised went to Steve's camp program. He loved the wilderness and yearly took a big group of tough inner-city kids camping for ten days in Algonquin Park.

The years slid by and Charles's firm got to its 20th anniversary; it was now well established and profitable. Ashleigh was the mother figure for a young staff, Charles the beloved founder and keeper and enforcer of a culture of respect and teamwork. He worked hard but it came easily. He was a natural in the business and he gave his mother Peggy full credit. He survived the untimely death of his wife and cherished the time he had with his grown daughter, whom he loved taking out and having people think the tall young brunette was his date.

But Hollie, who had become a real target for his considerable reserve of long unrequited affection, had eluded him and he could not understand why. She was a real challenge—why was his usual charm not working? Granted he had left her in the city for a few weeks when he was off at the cottage and had not even e-mailed her. But he had genuinely wanted to see her again. He was unlikely to get into a romantic relationship with another woman in her mid-thirties. He was attracted to Ashleigh, but she was his close colleague and off limits. So, the fact she wanted to take up with another guy did not cease to bother him. He would meet her again at some point, and it would have to be in the woodlot.

* * * * *

It had been almost two years since they had seen each other when one early spring Saturday he pulled up with Mabel to the place they used to meet at their old 11:00 a.m. time and sure enough the worn-out Camry was parked there and Hollie and Joe were just down the path when Charles got out. Mabel rushed ahead and was yelping and all over Joe. Hollie turned with a huge smile on her face. Charles caught up.

"Wow, is it great to see you!" Hollie was beyond happy.

"This is too wonderful—I had so hoped we'd meet again in the woodlot." Charles was beaming too, and gestured towards her. "Am I allowed?" She nodded and fell into his arms. They hugged fiercely.

They both said "I've missed you!" at the same time and laughed.

Hollie was anxious to update Charles as they strolled on.

"Warren, my squirrel guy, turned out to be the worst sort of cad," she started, looking embarrassed. "We moved in together into an apartment in the city. I had a small study to work in and we were okay for the first year. But I should have known something wasn't right. Joe never warmed up to him. Dogs know."

"Thank God he likes me," Charles chimed in.

"That was never in question, and by the by, so did I… anyhow one weekend when he was away at some writers' conference in Montreal, I was lonely and decided to phone his room at the hotel. I seldom called when he was away. To my surprise a female voice answered with, 'Hi, Mom!' Obviously she had been expecting the call. 'No,' I said firmly, 'It's Hollie, Warren's partner.' 'Oh!' she was obviously struck dead. 'Just a moment.' My sheepish guy was full of BS apologies and lies. I hung up. I forgave him that time. But not the next when he told me he was going out with an old friend for a beer, and I found a receipt for a very expensive dinner club in his jacket I was taking to the cleaners. Classic. Under my cross examination, he admitted he was with Shirley, the woman he had met in Montreal. That was it. I won't be lied to and two-timed. I told him we were through. Finito. The end. Now do we have a new beginning, Charles? *Please.*"

"If you insist. I suggest we get takeout and a bottle and retire to my house. Sound like a plan?" Charles was in heaven. Champagne from the liquor store and rotisserie chicken from around the corner.

They set the takeout meal out on the dining room table. Charles got fluted glasses and they popped the champagne and drank to each other and to their future. They got right back into easy conversation as if they'd never been apart. Hollie had met the great Canadian wildlife artist Robert Bateman at a gallery showing and was inspired to broaden her work to include wild animals, not just cute baby animals for children's books. She was anxious to show Charles some of her work.

Out of the blue, Charles asked whether she had ever been sexually assaulted. He had found out by asking several women that most indeed had been in some way, including his number two at the office, Ashleigh—a sad commentary on gender inequality, he thought. Indeed, she had a story that had them both laughing out loud.

"Funny you should ask. I think about it sometimes when I hear other women tell much more harrowing tales. Mine was more funny than harrowing. Want to hear?"

"Sure." Charles was all ears. She launched into the story with relish.

"There is an informal club of children's writers that meet occasionally and I attended one a few years ago at a not too elegant lodge in Muskoka. We all drank a lot, particularly George, a middle-aged man who was all over me. So, I excused myself early and went to bed. Lying there trying to go to sleep I heard a noise at the window. I looked up and saw a man removing my screen and boosting himself up and over the sill of the open window into my room. It was George, the drunken guy I had left a little while ago, determined to be amorous. He was on me in an instant, and I pushed him off the bed and onto the floor and told him to get out. He did. My sexual assault. It makes me laugh in thinking about it. I was on the ground floor, and he must have found out my room number and counted out the windows. Not bad for an inebriated older guy. I saw him the next morning and he didn't remember anything. Funny, eh?" They both laughed.

Charles found it amusing and told Hollie she was lucky that that was the worst she had ever experienced. She agreed.

"I wonder if you want to gently assault me now?" she said with a grin.

"Love to." He replied.

"This way, I presume…" she led him by the hand up the stairs into his half-lit bedroom. He turned on the bedside light. It was the same routine as the last time except that Hollie simply stripped down to her tiny panties before undressing Charles. He marveled at her perfect breasts glowing in the warm light of the small bedside lamp. She pulled him down on top of her, threw off her panties and put his hand between her legs and showed him how to pleasure her. This quickly aroused him. But she was not ready and directed the rest of the lovemaking to ensure she had an orgasm. Which she did and he came almost simultaneously inside her.

They lay side by side, exhausted.

"Did I tell you I'm off the pill?" She felt a bit guilty not telling him before. Even if it was unlikely he would have a condom. "Well, I guess we are in the hands of fate then. Do you think we just made a baby?"

"Well, if we did it was really good. Who knows? Would you be upset?"

"I don't think so. I really want to be with you for a long time. There's been a big hole in my life these last years."

"Mine too. But it really only came to me how tight and happy we'd been when I moved back to the neighborhood and started walking Joe in the woods. And I threw it all away."

"Well, I let you."

"True, you didn't fight back when I said I might move on."

"I guess I knew there was no point in arguing when you have made up your Dutch mind—right?"

"Well, I've made it up this time and we're staying together. Try and change that!"

"Great! I get lucky, No fight from me, we're for it, as you'd say."

"We sure are."

And she was right. They started the process of moving in together. Hollie had signed a monthly lease in the suburban apartment she had moved into after leaving Warren, so she gave notice and Charles started a major cleanup and decluttering of his house in preparation for the great day. Meanwhile, she stayed with him most nights and they did not tire of each other or the regular joy of sex. The dogs slept together downstairs on a huge bed they bought for them. Joe was having trouble on stairs and Hollie's vet wanted him to have an operation. She was resisting.

Peering into each other's most secret souls did not uncover anything that gave either pause. They found out they shared a lot—even down to both dads blaming the dog for farting when in fact it had been them. This was a tradition they both continued. And they heartily agreed that some of the finest people they knew were dogs.

Meeting with their parents went well. Charles had to see Mr. Jansen's nearby fully equipped cabinet making shop and was duly impressed with how clean and organized it was. And his mom, Peggy, was impressed with Hollie's tale of the role of the Canadian colonel who had liberated his town in helping set up the shop. She offered tea in bone china cups in her well-decorated apartment in the retirement home and was direct asking Hollie pointedly about children. Hollie allowed it was a "consideration." She seemed satisfied, and gave Hollie a polite hug as they left. Hollie saw a lot of Charles's strengths and appeal in her.

Chapter Seven

Moving day came and went and while a lot of Hollie's furniture ended up in the basement, her antique desk made it into the living room. Her big bed turned out to be newer than Charles's and came into his bedroom. And of course, her clothes joined his in his newly uncluttered closet. Her studio was set up in Sammy's old bedroom, which luckily had a south facing large window and she was very pleased.

Her kitchen pots and pans turned out to be much better than his 30-year-old set and so replaced them. She had modern crockery and it joined his more old-fashioned traditional wedding present set. Altogether their getting together improved both their living arrangements.

She had some framed art of some of her best original animal illustrations which Charles welcomed to their walls which had only a few of his paintings in any case.

Slow Love

With the addition of Hollie's framed family photos, it was starting to look like their house at last.

As the weeks moved on Hollie started to feel a bit strange and wondered if she was pregnant. It didn't take much to find out she was. That first night and subsequent ones had been too good.

She had been working in her studio at her apartment and came to Charles's house to meet him coming home from the 6:00 p.m. train.

They embraced and she held him, looking straight in his eyes.

"Okay, ready for this? I'm pregnant!"

"Oh my God. It's sure been fun getting you there. I'm delighted." And he held her tight. For a good thirty seconds.

"Well, you proved yourself, Mr. James." She was radiant.

"So, when are you due?"

"I'm just six weeks in—so looks like it was almost the first amazing night that did it!"

"How perfect. I'll never forget it. Nice to know, too."

They were not a particularly chatty couple, since they were sufficiently close they often thought the same thing at the same time. This was an endless source of joy for them. Even in talking about their coming parenthood and what was in store for the boy (as it turned out), they were in sync. He would first go to Montessori, then they would send him to the local public school which was walking distance from their house. Then to the private day school. The dogs would be fine—both were good with children.

Charles wanted to expose Hollie to his work at East Downtown Neighbourhood Services. It was part of who he was. "Giving back," as he would explain to her. So, one day they went downtown to have lunch with Steve, the tough youth worker. He was not hard to set off talking about his problem kids and the failures and successes he had trying to convince them to make the right life choices. She told Charles after how revealing it was: "We have no idea how poor people live and the challenges their kids face." She made a mental note to see if there was anything she could do to help these kids.

One key aspect of Charles's life still evaded her. His daughter. As luck would have it, before she moved in with Charles, Hollie was out in the woods with Joe one lunchtime when along came Mabel with a tall young brunette. Hollie knew it was Sammy and she was about to meet her for the first time.

Hollie was never shy. "Hey, you're Sammy, aren't you?" she said when they were at talking distance and the dogs were already greeting each other like long lost friends. "I'm Hollie. It's about time we met."

"Well, hello." It was a warm greeting and the tall well-built Sammy had Charles's crinkly smile. "I don't know why Dad has kept us apart. Particularly since you're moving in, right?"

"Yup. We're going to keep house together and the dogs will cohabit too. We all are very happy."

"I'm so glad. Sorry I won't have to walk Mabel anymore. I'll miss that but maybe we can meet. Anyhow, Dad has lost years since you guys got together. He looks great."

"He should. I make him go -to the gym. And we both have bicycles now."

"So do I. We'll have to do a proper ride someday."

"Yes, and just let me know when you want to join me in a lunchtime walk with the two four-legged lovebirds!"

They walked on together chatting easily, to the relief of both. Hollie did wonder if Sammy knew she was pregnant, and decided not to say anything this time.

It turned out they had a lot in common. Both were fit and working on staying that way. Both obviously Charles watchers. Sammy had a few Charles cottage stories to share. Like the last time he had a huge water ski wipe out.

"He wants me to come up for a weekend," Hollie mentioned, "Next weekend in fact. Will you be there?"

"Sure, if I'm invited. I do have a new boyfriend."

"Is it serious?

"Not yet."

By this time, they had done a short loop into the valley and Hollie was back at her car. They and the dogs parted, and Hollie decided to make sure Sammy came to the cottage that weekend with or without the boyfriend. It just was right that they be good friends.

Charles was a bit sheepish when Hollie told him they'd met by accident. He had planned a formal dinner. Just as well, he thought. He'd always been apprehensive about how they'd get on. Probably unnecessarily.

Hollie was nervous about the weekend. Not a Muskoka person for sure. She was not even a very good swimmer. And the only time she had been in a boat was in a cheap little kayak they had bought on one of their camping trips to Lake Simcoe when she was a teenager.

Piled into the Lexus with the dogs that Friday early in the afternoon "to beat the traffic," she admitted as much to Charles.

"At least I can have a run. Where at your place?"

"Sammy runs all the way from our cottage to the main road. It's about 3K, a good hilly run. Oh, by the way she and her boyfriend will be up tomorrow."

"Good. I'm sure we'll all get on. We'll have to tell her I'm pregnant."

"That should be interesting."

Slow Love

It was the end of a long wine-soaked BBQ hamburger dinner on the patio Saturday night. Hollie announced as only Hollie could by pulling up her T shirt, showing a slightly rounded tummy and saying, "In case you hadn't noticed, this is not the flat tummy I work so hard to keep that way. We're going to have a baby and I hope you are as thrilled as we are. Sister Sammy!"

Sammy found her announcement so original and fun that she could not help breaking into applause.

"Way to go, Dad!" She exclaimed. "I wondered if you still had it in you. Obviously, you do. I'm thrilled for you both. About time he became a father again. Thanks, Hollie."

"It was a pleasure, believe me." If only she knew how good they were in bed, she thought.

The weekend was easygoing "No rules here," Sammy explained as dishes piled up. There was no discussion about who would do them. They all just pitched in. Meals occurred when someone felt like providing them, and Hollie decided to do tuna fish sandwiches with chopped pickles Sunday at lunch. They were a hit. Charles took her for a long fast boat ride around the lake, the dogs up front their noses in the wind. Hollie loved the wind filling her hair and she looked with delight back at the foaming wake spreading out in an ever widening 'V' behind them. He spent a couple of hours Sunday afternoon with his easel and oil paints on the patio, stabbing at a large canvas of a pine tree. "I'm in my lone pine phase," he explained to her. Her art was so refined and precise she couldn't relate, "My God, you use a lot of paint!" He just loaded up a large brush with dark green and jabbed away at the branches of the pine tree.

She sunned on the dock in a red one-piece bathing suit that showed off her great figure, perfect long legs, and the tiny bulge in her tummy. Turned out Sammy was a wonderful looking young woman too. Not as fit and hard as Hollie, taller and fuller bodied with larger breasts strapped loosely into her bikini top. John, the boyfriend, looked at her lecherously. He was skinny and pale but a nice enough person and ready to pitch in. Charles was tanned and very masculine, Hollie thought. She was happy.

Mabel seemed to be teaching Joe how to chase the wily chipmunk and noisy, teasing red squirrel. Joe was perfectly at home and despite his hip issues was in and out of the water chasing a ball.

There was even an incident that proved how bonded the dogs were. Late in the afternoon the dogs had gone off into the woods above the cottage chasing after something and the gang on the dock were surprised after an hour or so to see Mabel coming back alone, whimpering and looking very concerned.

Slow Love

"Where's Joe?" Charles bent down and asked Mabel looking right into her eyes.

She barked and bounded off up the hill with Charles and Hollie, who had to find her shoes, in hot pursuit. They lost her but could follow her barking and finally there she was standing over Joe who was moaning softly, his front paw caught in a rock. Charles heaved it up and Hollie got him free. He staggered to his feet.

"Seems he'll live," she said, kneeling down and stroking him soothingly.

"Good rescue job, Mabel!" Charles was patting his dog who was licking Joe's paw adoringly. "You know we might have taken a long time finding him without Mabel."

"No doubt about it, she's a hero!" Hollie and Charles hugged the wagging dogs and laughed.

And so it was that the story of Mabel rescuing her boyfriend Joe became a cottage legend.

Later that night after the boys crashed with a bit too much wine and toasting the dogs, Hollie and Sammy went and sat down together at the dock to look at the stars and discuss men.

"John is such a kid," Sammy admitted. "He's in his thirties but spoiled and has no ambition. Still lives at home. And what a home. His mom dotes on him. But he's gentle and not too demanding. I sort of envy your relationship with Dad. It's so, how can I put it? Grownup."

"Well, we did put some effort into getting to know each other before we committed. It took a long time—we called it slow love—and I had to go out with a young asshole who cheated on me to appreciate what a decent caring person your dad was. Do you know he brings me breakfast in bed every Sunday? And he feeds the dogs and walks them in the morning, so I don't have to get dressed. That's caring, eh?"

"That is. Wow! Can I ask you who fell in love first, you and dad or the dogs?"

"Oh, the dogs for sure. We waited and pondered and fussed. Wanted to be sure. Then I broke it off for my interim fling. Then we met walking the dogs again, and eventually I moved into his house. Your house, I guess."

"Yes, I gather my old bedroom is your studio. I was only in it when I came home from college. But it is nice and bright—south facing."

"Best studio I've ever had. So how is your love life?" Hollie was being her direct self, and Sammy did not mind.

"Oh, John is a bit of a technology nerd but loves my boobs. Can't keep his hands off them. Thankfully, he's gentle and kind. And very smart. But he will not have my nice flat as his place for a long time. I'm not going to give up my freedom and independence easily."

"Well, I'm not as well-endowed as you. But as your dad says: 'more than a handful is a waste.' They will grow now, though. A friend of mine who had two babies and has smaller breasts told me she missed how big they got! Anyhow, enough boob talk. So, what do you do?"

"I'm in PR like my dad. Worked at his firm summers during college, so it was foreordained I'd be in the business. I like it. Lots of variety. I work for a clothing store chain and a large white tablecloth restaurant chain. We'll have to have dinner there together. We'll be well looked after."

"I'd love that!" And Hollie meant it. They bonded that night under the stars. And the next morning when thy ran together to the main road. Hollie was secretly pleased that she found it easier than the younger girl. Whatever, a relationship that could have been challenging and difficult was easy and rewarding. And would become more important as Hollie and Charles faced major life trials.

* * * * *

Pregnancy was a challenge. It was not an easy one. Hollie was almost forty and her doctor had warned her she would experience more aches and pains than a younger woman. He was so right. She had to stop training since her joints ached. It affected her sleep and hence Charles's. And at five months she was getting big and that affected their precious sex life. She had happily passed the trimester in which she might have miscarried, which she knew was more common for women her age. But so was a later and more traumatic stillbirth which gave her nightmares. So concerned that she became hypersensitive to any change or reduction in the movement of the baby in her stomach.

Her anxiety transferred to the dogs who became less lively and spent more time lying at her feet. And Joe's hip problem was worsening. She might have to let him have the operation after all. As for Mabel, her caring nature showed through and she was the one up on the sofa with her head on Hollie's shoulder. She was super affectionate with Hollie, and Joe, who was not as able to jump up on the sofa, was a bit jealous. She never ceased to be amazed about how the two canine friends sensed her moods and worries.

She shared her anxieties with Sammy one late afternoon at their house. Sammy was sympathetic and a good listener. She and John were planning to get married at that time and being well over thirty herself she knew she faced some of the same issues.

"I can't stop thinking about how horrible it would be if my baby dies inside me. Can you imagine that?" Hollie started looking very downcast.

"No frankly. But you must stop dwelling on the worst and start planning for the best. It's not like you to be so pessimistic."

"I know. I am so used to being happy go lucky and everything going my way. Should not have read up on giving birth at forty. It's full of all this horrible stuff. At least I didn't miscarry."

"How is Dad taking all your worries?"

"I guess I'm Dutch and don't want to burden him. But it is ruining our sleep. I'm hurting and between nightmares and aches don't sleep much. Maybe we should move into separate rooms so he can sleep."

"Oh don't. Gotta keep human warmth. And I'm sure Dad offers that. Right?"

"Yes, we hug a lot. And he has amazingly warm feet—unlike mine. But sex is getting more difficult and less enjoyable for me. Be forewarned—pregnancy is a challenge to marriage. Sounds like a song!" They did a little riff on it and laughed. It changed the somber mood.

Weeks went on and the pregnancy seemed normal. Lots of kicking and Hollie liked telling everyone and having them feel "the life in my body." Mabel's attempts to get her head on Hollie's lap were becoming difficult and she was not amused. Joe's hip issue was not improving, and he almost fell on the steps one morning and Hollie was about to make the big decision. But then he seemed better. Walks were shorter and that suited her as she had less energy for long lunchtime walks with the two dogs, even if Sammy joined them occasionally.

Christmas came and went. Peggy, Sammy and John, and John's sister Sandy filled out what became a big family goose dinner, cooked and served by Charles and Hollie, with a Christmas stollen for dessert in the Dutch Christmas Eve tradition. It was a warm and happy evening and the dogs got special treats and wore big red ribbons. They both got new squeaky toys, and Mabel ran around tossing her rabbit with great joy. Old Joe just gnawed away at his monkey. After dinner Charles played DJ and they all danced.

Hollie got bigger and hated what she called her "waddle." But she kept up her humor and Charles kept telling her how beautiful she was, "with all your hormones in top gear."

Then one rainy cold February evening after Charles had cooked a chicken dinner, Hollie exclaimed. "My baby isn't moving. Charles, come and put your hand on my stomach. Oh my God!" He did and could not feel any stirring of the fetus. They looked at each other in horror and tears started streaming down Hollie's cheeks. The dogs were at her feet moaning quietly.

"We have to call your obstetrician right away." Charles took charge. Dr. Lowe told him not to panic. She could come into the hospital in the morning and they would do an MRI. Sometimes the fetus just went quiet. But the procedure would tell them for sure.

Slow Love

Neither slept that night. They discussed the future over and over. Should they prepare for the worst? Would this be the end of their dreams of having a family? Could they get over it? They might have to. Charles tried hard to be confident, but it was an act and Hollie knew it. They both felt they were staring over a huge abyss waiting to be knocked into it. They shared this exact terrifying image almost simultaneously. This being almost in each other's minds was a remarkable feature of their relationship and of great value in situations like this.

"It's wonderful to know we are suffering the same way." Hollie said after they had admitted to having the same fear.

"Yes. But we're not going to go over the edge. Are we?" Charles said, trying to offer some comfort.

"Not if we're really together through this." She said, squeezing as close to him as she could and holding his hand tightly.

Then as ill-timed misfortunes tend to pile up, they suffered another simultaneous dramatic turn of events. Early the next critical morning they heard a crash and a yelp. Charles bounded up and there was Joe at the bottom of the stairs having great difficulty getting up. Hollie was soon right behind him.

"Oh my God. He'll have to be operated on. We'll take him to the vet on the way to the hospital. Shit! I left it far too long." And she got down as best she could and comforted Joe. He was barely able to be helped up. Mabel was licking him sympathetically.

They then got going far too early for the hospital appointment at nine-thirty. They were both exhausted. Quiet. Hollie had to fast for her procedure, so Charles didn't eat either. "That's what 'in it together' means." She appreciated the gesture. Hollie called the vet. It was going to be expensive, but Joe was going to recover fully. They tried to distract themselves by reading the paper and listening to the CBC news. Joe was huddled in a corner with Mabel. They knew something difficult was up.

They left at eight-thirty and went to the vet, which was on the way to the hospital. Charles took Joe out of the back seat in his arms. He was barely able to hobble in. They were at the hospital welcome sign-in at 9:20 a.m. and redirected to the gynecological clinic on the second floor of a low building across from the main hospital. There they checked in for Dr. Lowe and waited anxiously.

He was a white-haired heavyset middle-aged man who approached them with a warm smile and said,

"Hello. I know you're terribly worried but come in and I'll examine you and then we'll do an MRI. It's not unheard of that a fetus at your stage becomes inactive."

Slow Love

Charles had to wait outside the examining room and could feel sweat on his back. Finally, the doctor came out with Hollie, both smiling.

"I can hear a heartbeat." And the weight was lifted, though not entirely. There might be complications in the way the baby was positioned in the womb. But the MRI would tell him. If that was the case a birth might have to be induced. It would be a very premature baby, but there would be no danger.

The two fell into each other's arms for what seemed like a long time. The doctor watched, embarrassed.

"Okay. Let's get you across the street for an MRI. Here's a requisition. You should not have to wait. I have marked it urgent. They will send me the pictures and I'll call you right away.

And so their personal saga played out.

They got the call that afternoon. The baby was in an odd position and would have to be induced. He would be a month premature, but that was not that unusual. "He would have to go to into an incubator where you'll be able to touch him but not hold him right away. You'll probably be able to breastfeed him after a few days. But the nurse will get you to pump milk for him right away. I'm sure it will be fine. He looks good in the MRI, which I will email to you. I'll email you instructions to come for the birth tomorrow later in the day." He was obviously making it sound routine, which for Hollie and Charles it was anything but.

They were listening to him together on the wireless phone extensions. They clicked off and Hollie threw her arms around Charles and whispered, "That's what you get for marrying an older woman!" She paused for a moment. "Oh damn, we forgot about Joe! I'll call."

The operation had gone well but Joe was having a reaction to the anesthetic. The vet was a bit worried but told Hollie to call the next day. He'd likely be okay.

"Have to worry about me and the dog getting through tomorrow!" she said ruefully to Charles. "It never rains; it pours. God, I wish we were both younger."

"Well, he is an older dog, but you—an older woman!?" and he grabbed her still very firm young bum. "Not down here!" This broke the tension.

They had a day to put in and happily Sammy came by and distracted them with her marriage plans which were odd to say the least. They wanted a low-key backyard wedding at Charles and Hollie's place. And a professionally-catered BBQ dinner. On a Saturday in May. They figured about thirty people. Everyone could sit scattered about the house, deck, and backyard. A few rentals and a barman. No big deal. And their baby would be the star, no doubt.

"Oh, and we are trying to get pregnant—no time to lose, eh?" she exclaimed.

"You'll be fine." Charles said and they both gave her a big hug.

So, time to go to the big suburban hospital. Charles felt like a third wheel as Hollie was whisked away for pre-op, barely looking back. He found the most comfortable chair in the waiting room nearby and settled down with his cell phone. He was nervous but had managed not to show it that day. Hollie had told him he was her rock. He felt more like a limp old sock but was glad he hadn't shown it.

Ninety minutes later, the large, tall doctor emerged, took off his gloves and shook Charles's hand. "He's fine, a bit over five pounds and is in an incubator and being well looked after. Your wife will be a bit a bit blue and is in the recovery room. I'll take you."

Hollie said, "Tell me he's going to be to be alright… please. I can't hold him—they whisked him away." She looked up at him pleadingly. She was very pale.

"He will be—this is pretty routine now. If you're okay, I'll get a wheelchair, we can get a nurse and go and see him."

They looked through the glass and there was this tiny little thing all curled up in a clear container with the nametag: "Hollie Jansen." He had a breathing tube in his tiny nose and tabs on his chest to take his pulse. His heartbeat looked strong in the monitor.

The nurse said Hollie could feed him after a day or so. She wanted milk and Hollie had to pump. Happily, milk came from her now full-sized breast which Charles admired.

Finished, she looked at Charles and exclaimed, "We forgot Joe! Phone and see if he's okay."

He was and could be picked up in the morning.

"That's one life started and another improved. Not bad for one day, eh?"

"We are so blessed. I think we are just on a cloud and it's going to be sunshine for the rest of our days. Thank God we got together."

"Thank God for the dogs, or we wouldn't be here."

"Yes, to Mabel and Joe and whoever that is in the incubator. New life, new love, eh? And we have to find a name—this is embarrassing! As is the fact we did not get married." And she took a water glass off the side table and clinked it with her nails. Charles found another in the bathroom, and they toasted their future in water.

That day was full of good omens indeed. The next day they decided to name their boy Christopher and to get married that spring with Sammy and John. The nametag was changed on the incubator.

Chapter Eight

May 25th that year.

It turned out to be a double backyard wedding, Sammy acted as Hollie's bridesmaid, and she acted as hers. It was a family affair with Charles's mother Peggy all done up with a big hat and the Jansen parents in their shiny Sunday best. Their son Peter, wife Dawn and two kids Daphne and William were well turned out and between these toddlers and Hollie's noisy baby there was enough to keep a local teenage babysitter very busy. Sammy had a couple of attractive female friends from work, as did Charles his gorgeous number two Ashleigh and her husband. And Hollie invited her favorite author Jonathan Macintosh, a tall, charming Scot, and his wife Grace. The Majors, Sammy's new in-laws, turned out to be a staid but loving pair and they brought their other offspring, a tall stringy 25-year-old daughter named Sandy.

The backyard had a few rows of rented white chairs set up and Hollie had bought a couple of large white floral displays that framed the small wedding parties.

On the great day both brides looked suitably ravishing, Hollie in a slim form-fitting white satin knee-length dress, white stockings and heels, and Sammy in a revealing off-the-shoulder scalloped dress in white taffeta. The men were in light summer suits and colourful silk ties and matching silk pocket handkerchiefs. John had not polished his brown oxfords shoes but was otherwise well groomed.

Hollie and Sammy dressed in the main bedroom of the house together. Both the dresses were tight and demanded a bit of wriggling to get into, and that created lots of giggles.

"This is so cool getting married together. I'm so happy for both of us." Hollie was effusive.

"You got it. Imagine daughter and lover getting hitched the same day. It's so, so good. And to think I told Dad once that I didn't need him to marry someone who could be my sister…and what I have in you is something so much better!" Finally zipped in, they embraced. Old Joe the lab was curled up on the bed with Mabel, totally disinterested. But they followed them down to join the guests and circulated and greeted everyone. Then bridesmaid Sammy leashed them to be ready to be brought down the aisle following Charles and Hollie.

Instead of some traditional wedding march for coming up the grassy aisle, Hollie and Charles wanted Bob Marley's "One Love" on a boombox. So, they bopped down the grass to meet the hired Anglican priest singing, "Let's get together and we'll feel alright!" Sammy and John used the same music and by that time everyone was shouting "One love" on cue. Charles and Hollie gave each other a big wink when the priest intoned "love and honour until death do you part…" They had finally pledged love to each other the evening the baby had come home. Charles had a ring and proposed formally to Hollie the next day.

"We are so for it," he had said, "so we have to go all the way."

To which she got back with a wicked smile, "If you insist!"

The priest blessed Mabel and Joe at the end of the vows while the bride and groom embraced, saying, "bless these faithful friends of the bride and groom whose love for them has been important to their marriage." They stood still beside Sammy, tails wagging. They knew this was their moment. But not the last.

Sammy and John were next, and Hollie was bridesmaid. It went smoothly. Vows accomplished, the two wedding parties went up the cedar stairs to the small deck overlooking the backyard to make a few toasts and speeches, followed by the dogs. The hired waiter had popped the champagne and had a big tray of fluted glasses offered to the wedding parties and the guests.

Charles started by welcoming all to their house and then could not resist talking a bit about their meeting.

"I have to say this wedding would not be happening if it were not for the dogs who met and liked each other and sort of forced us to meet, which took us to where we are today. They were truly bonded to each other from the start, proven when Mabel led us way into the woods at the cottage to save Joe whose paw was caught in a rock. They set the tone for the human bonding that followed between Hollie and me. Let's raise a glass to Mabel and Joe!" The surprised guests did just that and both dogs standing at the edge of the deck looking down cocked their ears as their names were shouted by the group.

"But of course, I am supposed to toast the bride. That's easy. She made her mind up to get back to me after a brief interlude with another man. We met again in the woods with the dogs where we first got together. And once her Dutch mind was made up, that was the end of it. As we used to say, we were for it. And how truly lucky I am to have this beautiful, energetic, edgy and accomplished woman as my partner, mother of my son and finally wife.

To Hollie, my forever holiday!" Clink clank and it was Hollie's turn.

She leant down and got old Joe's paws up on two posts of the deck's railings.

"Here's to Joe," she said, "my longest boyfriend and most loyal. Until that is, I met Charles. I didn't know they still made nice men. But here he is. Thanks, Peggy, for teaching him to respect and cherish women and especially the woman—me that is. He is polite and attentive and he must have got that from you, too. What a change from the men I daresay Sammy and I had to put up with for so long." She turned to Sammy, who was nodding. "Anyhow, what can I say, this old dog and this woman just love this slightly older man! Here's to Charles!" Clink clank.

John and Sammy did fine. In fact, Sammy's dwelling on what close friends she was with Hollie was very touching and very sincere—so much so that Hollie teared up and almost streaked her mascara.

They swept down the stairs with the dogs to the back lawn with phones flashing as their friends and family snapped photos. It was a warm simple reception on a warm early spring day.

The two couples and two dogs honeymooned at the cottage. Charles and Hollie would go to the Netherlands later in the summer. Although blackfly season was just starting, they spent most days on the dock where a light breeze kept them away. Charles gave Hollie canoe lessons and she was a fast learner, joining him in his red canoe before breakfast every morning for a forty-five-minute glide around the next bay. The dogs waited patiently on the dock and as thy glided in wagged and moaned with delight. It was a wonderful quiet and reinforcing daily routine.

"I'll make a Muskoka girl out of you yet!" he was fond of saying. She even gamely jumped into the still very cold lake with Sammy one warm afternoon to prove it. Charles had secretly bought her her own new paddle and that night did a mock investiture by blessing her on the shoulders with it and pronouncing her officially a member of the Order of Muskoka. They all laughed and toasted her. The dogs howled with all the excitement.

* * * * *

A year later

Just as Charles and Hollie were finally getting used to having a tiny baby son crawling about the house, lying on one or other of the very patient dogs and tugging ears, another event put their marriage to the test.

Charles was now over sixty and suffered from high blood pressure for which he took medication daily. But it remained high and one Saturday after their walk in the woods with the baby carriage and dogs, he doubled over with severe stomach pain. Hollie had to persuade him to go to the emergency room ("Oh it's nothing," "It must be serious, you can barely stand up!"). So, baby seat and baby in the now aging Lexus and off they went. Luckily, it was quiet, and the triage nurse suspected a serious condition and in ten minutes the intern was feeling his stomach. With a worried expression, he told them he feared it was a burst aortic aneurysm which would have to be operated on quickly. It could be life threatening, he said in a low voice.

He was wheeled immediately to have an X-ray and minutes later the intern was back stating his diagnosis was correct. He would find the on-call surgeon and they would operate hopefully within the hour. Hollie was perched in terror on a small chair in the curtained-off cubicle, holding the sleeping Christopher. Charles was lying on a gurney doubled in pain but had been put on a n IV drip and was receiving a strong painkiller, a nurse had assured her. He was not talking, adding to Hollie's worry. She called Sammy on her cell and brought her up to date. She said she would be there as fast as she could and would take the baby. Hollie was determined to stay with her husband. Thank God for Sammy who appeared in 15 minutes, puffing. She embraced Hollie and took the baby, assuring her not to worry; she would go to the house and stay and look after Christopher and the dogs as long as she had to. Hollie teared up with thanks. "It will be alright," Sammy said as she was leaving, "Good thing you got him here quickly."

Hollie wasn't sure. She had never been in a life and death situation before. And her beloved man, so helpless and in such pain. That was so unusual for him. Would she now lose him just as their new life was becoming so wonderful? Would he get the care he needed? The hospital had taken over. Seemed like a machine she knew nothing about was in full motion. A handsome Chinese man swept in, Dr. Chu the surgeon. Trying to be comforting, but obviously worried that everything would be ready. "We have to operate as soon as we can. We have two emergency surgeries and have to wait just a bit for the operating room. We'll take him for pre-op in a minute or two. You can come upstairs to the surgery floor and wait. Should be a couple of hours maximum. I'm hopeful."

Yikes thought Hollie. That's the best I'll get. She had the worst feelings. She followed the gurney being wheeled by an orderly down seemingly endless corridors and up in a big elevator. There was a drab green waiting room with a couple of elderly people in it where he told her she could wait, and it was goodbye Charles.

Would she see him again? She was determined to know what the risk was and searched aortic aneurysm on her phone. She learned that the most common type of aortic aneurysm is an abdominal aortic aneurysm, and that without surgery, the survival rate is twenty percent. While it can be fatal, for those who make it to a hospital there is a fifty percent chance of survival.

She could feel her heart beating faster. She felt very alone and her whole life at stake. All they had worked on together and the love-built life they shared now in peril. Why? Why Charles? Yes, reading on she could see that high blood pressure and smoking were contributing factors. But they thought they had it under control. They had talked about him being older and something happening to him, which she had dismissed. But he insisted they make wills, and he took out another insurance policy. I am too young to be a widow, she thought. And then and there she decided if worst came to worst, she would not marry again. Never. There could not be another Charles. He was not replaceable. Period. *Why am I thinking this way?* She thought. *Why the hell did I google on my phone? I just must be confident and wait. His life and future are beyond my control. Accept it.* She tried. But teared up a couple of times.

Her cell rang and it was Sammy. She sniffled, "Yes he's in surgery. No, I read that if a burst aneurysm is acted on surgically quickly there is only a fifty percent chance of recovery. I'm in a fit. Our lives can't end like this."

"They won't. They can't. Trust me. Dad is strong. He's never sick. Doesn't smoke and only drinks moderately. Your got him there very quickly. It's a good hospital. Don't fall into the darkness."

"I'm afraid that's where I am. Is little Christopher okay?"

"He's gurgling away—gave him his supper and most went in his mouth. Dogs are whining for you but ate well. Everything is fine and John is coming over. You can stay as long as you have to."

Reminders of her daily life buoyed Hollie. "Thanks, you're a doll—really."

"If you need to be spelled off let me know and I'll be there in a flash."

Hollie breathed deeply and looked over at the old couple on the chairs across from her. They were watching her and had heard the conversation. He was white haired and handsome with a bristle white mustache under a strong large nose. He had a deep voice and sympathetic big brown eyes surrounded by wrinkles.

"Our son is in surgery and it's serious, too. Just have to have faith, I suppose," he said.

"I'm finding it hard given what the internet says about my husband's problem."

"Never look at it for health issues. I'm told it's always too depressing."

Slow Love

Turned out the son had had a bad car accident and was having various broken bones fixed. But he also had a serious concussion which was what was worrying his parents.

The sharing of suffering and worry calmed Hollie. She closed her eyes and concentrated on her breathing.

Finally, two hours later the small Chinese surgeon came around the corner, still in scrubs. She held her breath and her heart raced.

"We repaired the artery. He'll be okay. Lost a lot of blood. He'll have to stay a day or so for observation. We got it in time." He was obviously relieved.

She felt a huge weight lifted. She could live again. "Oh, thank God and thank you." She blurted.

She was ushered into his recovery room, cubicle number eighteen, and there he was all wired and tubed up, stretched out straight on his back like a corpse, barely conscious. She leaned over and kissed him on a very warm cheek.

"I love you so much and am so thankful we'll go on as before. For a while I wasn't sure." He obviously missed this and just groaned a bit and mumbled something. His eyes were barely open. Twenty minutes later, with Hollie still right beside him and a few inches from his head, those eyes opened, and "Hollie…" came out sweetly.

"I'm here. I'll always be here," She said, thinking it was a bit redundant. But it was what she felt.

She reached under the sheet that covered him and found his hand which was tight in a fist. She gently opened it up and help it tight. It was warm and she felt a slight tingle. The attraction from years ago was still alive and vibrant.

About eleven o'clock that night she finally realized that her sleeping husband did not need her and that she was beyond tired. She gathered her purse and slipped out of the hospital into a taxi and went home. The house was quiet. Sammy was on the cot in the baby's room, and both were sound asleep. The dogs were very excited and many kisses later she fell into her empty bed and dozed into a deep sleep in seconds.

The next morning, she awoke with a start. Where was Charles? This was the first time they had not been beside each other in bed for so long. The dogs were together in their huge puffy donut at the end of the big bed. She angled out of the bed and put her feet in her slippers. Then the horrible events of the day before came rushing back and she gasped. Was everything really alright? She hated herself for doubting that he would be okay. She read the note on her bedside table. Sammy had gone to the hospital and the dogs were fed, had been put out and come upstairs to be with Hollie. Baby was still asleep. She would be back in a couple of hours. She had called the hospital and he was not going to be released until the following day. She gave Hollie the room number. She could return to look after things. She'd taken two days off work. That angel, Hollie thought.

An hour later, Hollie dressed with Mabel rubbing against her legs empathetically. Sammy returned. Christopher was fed and playing on the floor with the dogs in attendance, after Sammy took them around the block, and Hollie was off to the hospital where a surprise awaited her. She got on the elevator on the second floor off the main entrance and there was a gurney with a patient on it from a lower floor with a very large orderly who eyed her, though she barely noticed. Then the orderly spoke up in a fairly loud voice, "Hey, Hollie! Hello, it's me, Bob!" Hollie looked up and sure enough his square set handsome face was beaming. He had the drop on her.

"I'll be damned. What are you doing?"

"What does it look like? I'm an orderly. New life. Took courses at the community college. Good job. Being useful. Still coach judo. You? I know you're married—saw it in the local paper. Got your guy, eh? Jonathon told me about the wedding."

"Yes." Hollie was stunned to remember that Jonathon had introduced Bob to her. How ironic. But Bob seemed like a new man, and obviously that's what he wanted her to think. She felt she had to explain: "But he was very sick. As was I—sick hearted—it was serious and I thought I'd lose him, but he'll be okay. Oh. This is my floor. Good to catch up with you. Sounds like life is good for you."

"It is. Bye. I'd love to see you…"

She didn't answer. It was all too much. Memories of him flooded back. Some not so bad. It wasn't my fault he loved me too much, she thought. But he did – he actually was still her old bear.

She was nervous entering Charles's room. He was less wired and tubed and was sitting up. His face was grey and there were strain lines around his tired eyes, but he was almost smiling as she came in.

"You are a sight for sore eyes, darling Hollie."

"You too—and you're on the mend, thank God."

"Seems so. I can come home tomorrow, but I'll have to take it easy for a few days."

"I'll have to keep the dogs off you. They'll be so excited. And the baby. We all will be in heaven to have you back."

"For sure." She had something to say that spoke to the depth of her love for him. "You know, we always said we'd had slow love. I was thinking, trees grow slowly and put down deep roots. So does slow love. And it took the thought of losing you for me to realize how deep my love for you is and always will be. There that's my speech today!"

Slow Love

He reached out to her and drew her close and kissed her.

"I could not have put it better myself. All I could think of when they put me under was you and how our lives together had to go on. And they will. They are meant to go on—together."

They talked for an hour about the baby, how wonderful Sammy had been, Hollie's latest assignment, which was now overdue, how wonderful the nurses had been—"But I hope not too wonderful!"—Hollie had intervened, having noticed a particularly beautiful young nurse at the nearby station. She did not mention running into Bob.

She might as well have, for the next day when she came around noon to take him home who should appear with the wheelchair to take him to her car but Bob. It was awkward. He said hello to Hollie and Charles recognized him and said, "Hello Bob, fancy running into you."

"I've changed my life," he replied, "I'm enjoying serving people and have to say I'm glad Hollie found a solid guy like you. She deserves the best, and I wasn't it a few years ago."

For once, Hollie was tongue-tied. Charles saw she was embarrassed. They were now in the elevator. "Well Bob, I'm sure I speak for Hollie when I say we're glad to see you relaunched in a meaningful job."

"And I have a girlfriend. Not as wonderful as Hollie. But pretty great."

"Come on, Bob, I'm sure she is just as wonderful as me. We wish you all the best."

"Thanks, well, here we are." At the main entrance Hollie's car was parked in the short-term section just across the circular drive. She went to get it, leaving Charles alone with Bob, who had something to get off his chest.

"Hey, I'm sorry I behaved like such a jerk trying to spoil your scene with Hollie by accusing you of that drug deal."

"No problem, and it didn't work!"

"No, it was stupid, but I guess it all worked out for you two."

"It sure did."

They drove home and got a hero's welcome from the dogs. The baby gurgled and life slowly returned to normal.

Chapter Nine

Five years later

Looking back over five years of married life, Hollie and Charles felt very blessed, even if Charles had lost some bounce after his aneurysm, having a baby then a toddler kept him active and amused. Sammy and John had a child, a girl, Julia, and there was a lot of back and forth between the families. Also, Jonathon and Grace had become friends, as had Charles's number two at the office the tall and beautiful Ashleigh and her equally good looking husband Barrie. There were lots of parties, BBQs, and cottage visits.

One day in the autumn when Charles was about to have a sixty-fifth birthday (Hollie had already had a 60th birthday five years ago – she called the big happy party a "blowout"}- Hollie received a worrying call. It was Charles's colleague Ashleigh.

"Hey Hollie, sorry to bother you but I'm a bit worried and wanted to share my concern with you."

Hollie wondered what it could be. "No problem—shoot."

"Well, it's Charles. He's tired, I think, and not as sharp as he used to be. I've noticed him making mistakes in his emails to clients and writing in general. Not like him. He is very sensitive to my comments when I catch these things. But I just wondered how his health was. Anything I should know about?"

"Not really. He does complain about lack of energy and was put on some supplements by his health mad daughter. I've noticed he goes to bed earlier and sleeps later. But no, nothing really in terms of health issues."

"Well, he is very important to the firm as you know so I thought I'd send him to a private clinic for an absolute full checkup. Is that okay with you?"

"Sure. That would be great. He isn't getting any younger, that's for sure."

"None of us are." Hollie knew Ashleigh was in her fifties and hated it. Her fiftieth birthday really hit her even if it was a great party.

That same year Hollie lost her beloved Joe. He was over 16 and quite pathetic. He had stopped eating, no matter what Hollie found for him. Raw beef and chicken, treats, nothing appealed to him and he wasted away. Hollie was beside herself and Charles was at a loss how to comfort her. Finally, with Hollie sobbing in the back seat holding him, they took him to the vet to be put down. She stayed with him and held him as the vet gave him the lethal shot. It seemed like the end of an era to both. Hollie had done a wonderful drawing of him. It was framed, Charles had a plaque made, and it was hung above the mantel. In an equally trying scene a few months later Mabel died unexpectedly one night. It was Charles's turn to carry her to the car and be with her in the back as Hollie drove them to the vet. He was also there when she was put down.

These losses of such faithful friends who had played such a large part in their life weighed heavily on both. They had been so much more than members of the family. They were embedded in their relationship from the beginning. And they were as happy a couple as Hollie and Charles, forever licking each other and cuddling. When Joe disappeared, for days Mabel wandered the house looking for him, moaning and sniffing his smells all over the backyard.

At the same time Hollie started to have sad moments thinking about the difference in age between her and the love of her life, and what it would be like as Charles got older. It was precisely his maturity that had attracted her to him years ago. Age is just a number, she had said, but it was getting to be a bigger one. As for Charles, he was becoming more concerned about this as well. It was hard to talk about since it really didn't seem to make much difference. He was still okay in bed. Whenever the age thing came up Hollie would remind him that he was "as good a kisser as ever." He had enough energy to play with Christopher and loved reading to him every night in his bed. But it was unlikely he'd be a hockey dad with the other fathers twenty years younger. Was that important? Wasn't their love for each other all that mattered? "Love is all there is…" she would think, humming the old Dylan song. In some ways it was an almost mystical union and they talked about it that way.

In the end both usually left it at that. Until one evening in bed before turning out the lights. That evening in bed, Hollie was concerned about Charles's checkup, which she was in the dark about and had to ask him.

"So, Ashleigh told me you had a big checkup at a private clinic? How did it go?"

"Well, generally okay but they did detect a bit of arrhythmia, which would explain why I am tired sometimes."

"Oh God. That is serious, isn't it? What are we going to do about it?"

"I'm going to see a cardiologist. Next week, in fact. I'll be okay."

"Oh shit. I guess heart issues are an age thing. We'll just have to get used to the fact that we're getting older."

"You mean I am—sorry, but that's what we took on. You know I may just have to cut back a bit on work. Thank God, you are still young."

"And we love each other that's all that matters, eh?"

"Right." And they snuggled together and kissed passionately.

But they both now lived in sort of an unspoken "what if" land, particularly Hollie. What if Charles became sick and took a lot of looking after. What if their sex life died? It was an important feature of their relationship. What if he had to retire—what would that do to him? His self-confidence would take a big blow. And what would he do to keep busy and fulfilled? Would he be around the house all the time? How would that affect their relationship? Would they have enough money? There was no pension at his private firm. Would he have to sell the firm?

Hollie thought of one of Charles's favourite Dylan songs, "Forever Young," whenever she was caught up in this worry land. As he got older, she saw it describing her duty to him to stay forever young.

She would—it would be her gift to him as he inevitably got older and more needy. She would continue to light up his life. She would, damn it!

And she did. As the years went by and his importance at work faded, as he retired and in much sadness packed up over forty years of hard work and so many clients, as he lost the daily joy of young employees who looked up to him as a caring boss, as he settled into their house and learned to live a new daily routine with a young son, there was always the good humour and loving care and attention of Hollie to keep him happy. And of course, his daughter Sammy, her growing daughter and her unstinting love and affection for him.

Hollie tried to make every day special. A special dish, a special activity with Christopher, a special evening with Ashleigh and her husband when he could catch up with goings on at the office. Charles's mom Peggy was getting very old. He called her every day and visited her at least once a week. He fixed up his studio in the basement, and many days the house would be still as Hollie and Charles executed much different scenes in two different parts of the house.

Hollie arranged that two mornings a week an attractive young female trainer would come to the house and make him do exercises. His heart condition remained stable, but his energy levels were low, and it annoyed him that he could not undertake the physical activities he used to—particularly at the cottage where they weekended from May to September. No more water skiing and only canoeing with Hollie, not on his own—on Sammy's orders.

Leaving the company he had founded was particularly difficult, even if the senior staff had bought him out, making retirement possible.

"God, it's tough to admit you can't really hack it at work anymore. But Ashleigh is obviously so much smarter than me now when it comes to ideas and management. She was kind pointing out the issues I had with work. She was right about it being time," he admitted to Hollie one day. He kept up his charity work with at-risk youth downtown, raising money for their summer camp and after-work mentoring, but that was about it.

"Look, we are going to make it a lot of fun. It will be good living together when I finally have you to myself at home," she said cuddling him. "A new life together, look on it that way and I have all the energy to make up for whatever you feel you lack. As long as you are still a good kisser."

"You know it is wonderful that you are still young and so with it. What a gift to me. Thank you. Now here's a proper kiss." And he proved he was still a good kisser then and there.

They soon decided they could not be without a dog for too long, and Christopher, eight by this time, wanted a lab. So, they spent a lot of time finding a breeder of chocolate labs and an adorable puppy, called Joe, of course, was soon wriggling around the house to everyone's delight. He was pure joy and an instant favourite with the dog walkers in the woods.

He was generally a good puppy and they kept him in his crate for the first few months. He was house trained after a month. But he had one fault which amused them at first, then became problem. He had a ravenous appetite and would eat everything. Small pillows had to be hidden since he tore them up with glee. And socks had some special appeal, particularly if they were Charles's and recently worn. Finally, one day they caught him actually eating and swallowing a sock. Hollie took him right off to the vet where he was made to throw up the disgusting semi-digested article. The experience was instructive and from then on, he left socks alone.

Charles had been out shopping when it happened, and Hollie told him about it when he got home.

"He must love you a lot to eat a sock that smells of you," she said. "But I think the experience of having to bring it up at the vet's cured him. He must have dug it out of the clothes hamper. Have to admit he's clever."

"He just can't get enough of me, I suppose." Charles responded."

"He's not the only one." And they embraced.

"You know, Charles," Ashleigh the truth teller said on one of her irregular calls to Charles, "I really don't feel very sorry for you with a beautiful wife, a smart young son, and an adorable puppy."

"I'm not complaining," Charles admitted, "but I do miss you and the office."

"We miss you too, boss." Ashleigh said firmly.

"That's what I wanted to hear."

And so the years went by. Christopher was at the local private school and doing well. Indeed, he did not take up hockey, so Charles was spared early morning trips to arenas near and far. He loved soccer, and in the winter spent his sports time in the gym. He ran with his mother at least three times a week. It was their special time together and they were out whatever the weather. Christopher had to admit to his friends that he did not have to slow down hardly at all to run beside his mother. "She's that fit," he would tell them proudly.

Charles aged "gracefully" as Hollie liked to, say. His mother passed away and Charles had to arrange the funeral. They had a catered reception in the church hall of the Anglican church she had attended. Hollie's parents were getting very old and were in a well-equipped quite luxurious home that she had chosen, not too far from where they lived. They visited often and Charles enjoyed having a scotch with his father-in-law, reminiscing about the war and coming to Canada.

Inevitably for Charles and Hollie, lovers turned into the best of friends. They still hugged a lot and held hands, but blue and other pills notwithstanding lovemaking lacked the excitement that it had once. Hollie did not complain. She was still fit and energetic, and her hair was full, framing a slightly lined face. "I smile too much," she would say about the lines around her mouth. Her big worry was about losing Charles as he aged and became less active. He fell in the bathroom one day and bruised himself badly. More worry. And he knew full well that his heart condition made him a prime candidate for a heart attack.

He shared his fears with Hollie. She laughed it off. "Hey, old man, stop being so morose. You're fine. You keep me happy—isn't that enough?"

Chapter Ten

He was just 71—Hollie was 51—when it happened. It struck him early one bleak cold Friday morning in February. Christopher had just left for school. Hollie was in a robe after making a quick breakfast for him. His bus came and went.

Charles was just getting up. Terrible chest pains, profuse sweating, and nausea. Joe was at his side making strange noises; he would not leave him alone. Hollie knew she had to call 911—who told her to give him an aspirin and that an ambulance was on its way. This was it and she was shaking and almost sick herself. What she had dreaded for several years was happening before her eyes. He was gasping for air, and she had to use all her strength to help him in his pajamas down the stairs to the couch with Joe following and leaping up beside him. In minutes the doorbell rang, and an attractive young man and woman were there with a stretcher and some equipment. They put him on the floor checked his heart—he was having cardiac arrest. They started trying to revive him, the male paramedic pushing on his chest rhythmically, while the woman held the stethoscope. Then she opened a big bag and out came a defibrillator which she hooked up, attached to patches on his chest. She started to jolt him. CPR continued. Charles was gasping, the colour was draining from his face. Joe was moaning in sympathy. Hollie watched in horror. There was nothing to say. They were doing everything to save his life. Was it working?

"Shouldn't we get him to the hospital, pronto?" Hollie asked fearfully.

"We do what we can here," the paramedic explained. "Hard to do this in the back of the ambulance and we're twenty minutes from the hospital."

Minutes ticked by and Charles did not seem to be responding. The paramedics looked very anxious.

"I'm not sure we can do more," the male paramedic said. "Better get him to the hospital." They got the stretcher from the ambulance and heaved him on to it and into the back of the ambulance. They drove off with the siren sounding. They asked her if she wanted to be with him, but she was in her flimsy nightgown and said she would follow as fast as she could.

Slow Love

She rushed upstairs and threw on jeans and a sweater, grabbed her keys and purse, backed the car out of the drive and in 15 minutes of nerve-wracked driving was parked at the hospital emergency department.

She told the nurse at the entrance her husband had been brought in by ambulance with a heart attack. Where was he? She could hardly speak.

"You are Mrs. James? We have a team still trying to revive him. You'll just have to wait." And she showed her into a seat among a line of other anxious looking people of all shapes and ages.

She tried to keep her hands from shaking and control her shallow breathing. She felt half-dead herself. Devoid of feelings. Her nerves took over. Was this it? The end of her dream life with this solid guy who loved her so much?

Next thing she knew, Sammy was beside her. She had called the house, found nobody home, which was unusual early in the morning, and called the neighbor who told her an ambulance had left the house with its siren going.

"Thank God you're here," Hollie said her voice shaking. "They were having trouble reviving him at home—now they are still working on him. I do fear the worst."

Sammy hugged her. "Well, you're not alone. The two people who love him most are rooting for him. Hope he knows."

"He was pretty well out of it from the time he woke up. It's horrible. I don't think I'll get to say anything to him…"

They held hands and finally a young intern came down the hall and found her.

"You are Mrs. James?" Hollie could tell by his expression that it was bad news.

"Yes, and this is his daughter."

"I'm afraid we couldn't revive your husband. He passed peacefully in no pain. He did not regain consciousness. I'm so sorry."

The two women were stunned and burst into tears.

"It can't be…" Hollie gasped. Sammy went pale and blurted,

"This is not happening!!"

But it was. The dream romance had ended. Hollie was a wreck for several weeks. She had no appetite and despite her son's urging ate almost nothing. She lost weight and started to look gaunt. Nevertheless, she threw herself into her exercises and her work. Christopher at age eleven tried to cheer her up, Sammy took her to her favorite Italian restaurant and tried to get her to eat a decent meal. It was very hard for Christopher and Sammy too. They missed Charles terribly. The three spent many tear-stained moments on the sofa hugging each other. The dog spent a lot of time looking for Charles.

Slow Love

Hollie was completely overwhelmed with regrets. So much they hadn't done together. So much still to talk about. And their son's growing up which he would never experience. These were the subjects of constant laments. And the worst thing—she had never been able to say goodbye to him.

Hollie just had to adjust to being a widow. A young one at that. It would take many months.

There was a funeral and Sammy took charge. Hollie had to appear at the funeral home for a simple little service where Sammy spoke eloquently of what a good man, father and husband Charles had been. Her daughter Julia and Hollie's son sat with her and took it all in. They would not forget this day.

What to do with his things? Hollie was superstitious and until Sammy gave her a bit of a talking to, she had left everything as it was. His stuff in the bathroom and clothes as he'd left them. There was a half-finished painting in the basement. His voice was on the answering machine for over two months. It was all too much to face the fact that he was not coming back. Eventually she did.

What was riveted in Hollie's memory and haunted her dreams was Charles flat on the floor of their living room, breathing what she now knew was his last breath. She had not said goodbye.

He lived on in her dreams, canoeing, laughing in the cottage's dining room. Loping through the woods with her and the dogs. Stopping at the sawed log and reminiscing. And when they went to the cottage with Sammy and family, she was convinced he was still there. And his ghostly presence did from time to time visit her, she swore. It did not communicate but was there, usually early in the morning when she was half asleep.

"I truly believe that he will never leave the place he loved," she told Sammy one summer day. "And I believe our love will never die."

"That is a wonderful thought. Hang on to it," Sammy said.

Charles had left Hollie with no financial worries. The house was paid off. He had a huge insurance policy and sufficient savings. And she was still earning a good living from her illustrations. Christopher was soon in his upper grades in the private school. And while she missed him terribly, she was not to be without male companionship for too long.

* * * * *

It started as spring was just showing its face, three months after the funeral. One day the phone rang in her studio. Joe was curled at her feet and perked up. It did not ring often.

"Hey Hollie, it's Bob. Hope you don't mind me calling?" He sounded different.

"No. But don't you have a girlfriend?" Classic cut-to-the-chase Hollie.

"Nah. She was too high maintenance. Not like you. Can we get together?"

Hollie was tempted. She was still so immersed in being in mourning. Maybe he would be a distraction.

"Sure. I'm not up for a date, but it might be good to catch up. Haven't been out of the house except for dog walks for a while."

A few days later a rather sharp noisy red Honda Civic rolled up to the James house and out stepped Bob in a very neat blue sweater, white shirt and tie, navy slacks, and shiny black oxfords. Hollie saw him coming up the walk from the living room and was amazed. A new man indeed, no more old truck and crummy baggy clothes.

She greeted him at the door, and they had a formal hug.

"God, what a change!" she blurted.

Bob looked her up and down in her neat red Bermudas and white shirt and cuffs over a soft pink cardigan. "You're as sharp and as good looking as ever. No change here." He looked pleased with himself.

"Thanks. But I'm an old widow. And it sure has been a long time."

"Nearly twenty-five years, I figure. A lot of whiskey under the bridge."

"That's for sure. So, gentleman Bob, where are you taking your long-ago ex?"

"Well, you said no date, so I thought that means no dinner but maybe we could go to that Italian place and sit at the bar and have a glass of wine. I like wine now—I'm off beer!" They drove in his fast little car to Italia on the main drag and perched close together on bar stools. He couldn't keep his eyes off her.

Bob had changed. He was easy to talk to and his job in the hospital had softened him, exposing him daily to people's saddest situations and traumas. He was good at recounting the camaraderie among the nurses, orderlies, and interns at the busy suburban hospital. He liked being in the emergency department where the action was fast and furious. He didn't have too much good to say about the older emergency doctors who tended to be very demanding and enjoyed being top of the heap. He was back at a community college taking nursing.

"I want to be a nurse practitioner, even if I'm a bit older," he told Hollie, who was taken in by his stories and obvious caring for those he worked with. She realized that he was her age—over fifty. Brave to go back to school, and she told him.

"Thanks Hollie," he said, moving closer to her. "You know you were always the one. I never forgot. In fact, changing my life was for you. Even if you weren't available."

"I don't know if I'm available now. Charles and I had a very special scene and I'm not sure I can ever replace it."

"I understand. But maybe we could see each other occasionally. I'd really like that." He was almost pathetic, she thought. Her old huggy bear remade.

They did get together. He had a bike and they'd go for rides. He invited her to go and see his judo kids at a local tournament. It was revealing to see how well he coached them and how much they liked him. Hollie thought it would be good for her Christopher to join the group. Despite his busy soccer schedule, he did go to the once-a-week evening session. He enjoyed the action, and he liked Bob. Christopher was lanky but tough, Bob assured her.

He worked his way into her life, but there was no physical side to their new friendship. She made it clear that she was not up for even hand holding, which he had tried.

Then bad luck struck her again. Bob had kept in touch with Jonathan who had introduced them years ago. And he and his wife had stayed friends with Hollie. One day he called.

"Hey Hollie, it's Jonathan. I'm afraid I have some bad news about our friend Bob. He's been killed in a bad car accident. Thought you should know. The funeral is this Saturday. I could pick you up and you could come with us. Sorry."

This burst of horrible news hit Hollie like a brick on the head. She felt faint. And a bit speechless. There was a long pause.

"Are you still there?"

She caught her breath. "Yes sorry. I'm just so shocked. First Charles, now Bob. I'm really not up for this."

"Well, sorry. I know how much he always liked you. Didn't stop talking about you over the years."

"I know, but we weren't really a number this time around. Just good friends. And he coached my son in judo."

"I know—a nice man now for sure. Sorry to lose him, especially that way. What a waste. Fast car."

"Well, it was nice to have a pal who was a man." And Hollie thought *the last one, I'm pretty sure*. She wasn't totally convinced it would be.

It almost was. She relied more and more on her friendship with Sammy. She would pour out all her sadness and her continuing love for Charles and his appearances to her and she would listen lovingly and try and soothe her. They would meet afternoons a couple of times a month before Sammy went off to collect her daughter at school.

They agreed that their relationship was hard for men to understand. That men just couldn't admit weakness to each other. It was easy for them and talking about the father and husband was a release for both. Sammy had had issues with her mom which drove her very close to her dad, who she could talk to about anything. This was very rare and her friends, most of whom had absentee uncaring dads, were jealous.

Hollie's appreciation of Charles was very different, and she loved talking about it to Sammy. He had been thoughtful and caring to a fault. She'd once taken a tumble off her bike when they were riding together. He had picked her up and quickly brushed her off, held her hand and walked her home, where he dressed her scraped leg and fussed over her so kindly and with so much worry, Hollie recalled. And they worked out everything about the house, their child, and all their plans together. For a trip to the Netherlands, they'd sat at her computer going over every detail together. Just like they had for theirs and Sammy's wedding.

"We were a real team," Hollie would say. "It was a miracle. And maybe I shouldn't be telling his daughter this, but our lovemaking was what we saw as a sort of mystical union. We became one. Now to tell the truth he needed instruction—from me, of course. But he was a good pupil and we made each other happy regularly into his last few years. We turned from real loves into best of friends. It happens. But the physical feeling remains."

"Lucky you," Sammy said one day when Hollie was going on about how close they were. "John is fine. But we may be entering into the 'best friends' era a bit sooner than I would have hoped. One thing I know we share though is that I do not find any other man attractive. Thank God. But what about your old ex Bob—did he turn your crank at all?"

"Not really. He had been good in bed. But Charles was entirely different. Gentle and caring and sensitive above all. I wasn't the slightest bit tempted by rough and ready, wham bang thank you ma'am Bob."

They both hooted with laughter at her description.

"I had a few of those," Sammy admitted.

When they met, they'd recall so many happy times at the cottage, parties with friends to which both couples invited the other, and the bad scenes some of their friends had been through. Nasty divorces, sad kids. They were both proud of taking time to make sure their marriage and partner choices were sound.

"We were both practical even if we were in love and slow love paid off," Hollie would say.

Hollie swore she had visits from Charles. And one day she decided to share with Sammy what amounted to a message from him from beyond the grave. It was a sealed letter to be opened only by her, which was inserted into his will. One day she brought it out and with a shaky voice read it to Sammy:

My darling Hollie,

I will be gone from your life when you read this. I wrote this when I knew that my heart condition was worsening and was worried that maybe I'd better put down my feelings for you before other parts of me became diminished as well.

My dad used to say that a young wife was either an old man's fancy or a young man's slave. Obviously, you were my fancy but so much more. We had such a profound partnership as well as being lovers. As you once pointed out we went the slow love route which meant we put down deep roots like a big strong tree. And we were careful, both having had less successful relationships before.

But the truth is I think it is lucky both of us were born with an enormous need to be loved and a terrible need to give. And I daresay until we met each other we scattered that need to some extent—or at least I did. Then I experienced the classic falling when we first met in the woods. I found the focus for that need and it stayed with me all those years and made it inevitable that we would get back to each other after your brief interlude as we used to call it. What could be better than that?

Then there was the unity of thought and mind we achieved. Almost thinking the same thoughts, the same way, at the same time. It was uncanny and actually annoyed some of our friends. It meant we seldom disagreed on anything. Quite an accomplishment.

And I do thank you for patiently making me into your good lover.

"Don't know whether I should go on," Hollie was embarrassed to go on reading.

"Hey I'm his daughter!" Sammy exclaimed. "I used to ask him how his love life was, and he would always say it was fantastic!"

Hollie continued:

> Even lately when I'm obviously not the man I used to be, I get a tingle when you touch me, or we hold hands. You are a pleasure engine for me. How lucky can I be as I got older and still had those amazing physical feelings.
>
> I don't have to tell you how sexy, talented and beautiful you are. Your smile warms a room. And that you chose old me when you could have had so many other great guys more your age always astounded me. But what we built so carefully and with such love and compassion and caring would have been hard to duplicate for sure.
>
> It's wonderful to believe you'll always love me even after I'm gone. You always said, "I am because you are." That defined me, too. If I can, I intend to visit you so watch out for me. Maybe I still am.
>
> Yours forever,
> Charles

"And he drew a big heart and many x's and o's. Sweet, eh?"

"For sure. What a letter. I bet you read it often."

"I do. It's in my bedside table. He is still around, I swear."

Chapter Eleven

Three years later Christopher had now graduated high school and was taking the train to university in the city every day. He was a good soccer player and looked like Charles, with a wicked grin and lots of charm. He had a good relationship with Hollie, and they talked about everything. He loved Joe the dog and walked him every weekend in the woodlot where so much of Hollie's life had been defined.

The cottage had been left to Sammy and Hollie so the two families spent many weekends and holidays there together. Christopher was charming with his younger cousin Julia who turned out to be a lovely young girl. Sammy got a dog, a standard poodle called Willow who got along fine with the older Joe. He remained the master water dog and chipmunk chaser.

Hollie was resigned to being without a man and having no more sex. She tried not to think about it. But Charles sometimes entered her dream life in a very real way, and she had sex dreams that left her terribly unsatisfied.

But life for her was about to change again when Jonathan Macintosh called her one day. She had not heard from he and his wife for a long time. He had a job for her and wanted to come over. She had a soft spot in her heart for him as one of her first clients. He arrived the next afternoon. Tall and handsome and energetic as ever, the big Scot gave her a big "How are you?" in his charming brogue and a warm hug, her first in a long time. Joe gave him a warm greeting—a good sign, Hollie thought. He had a manuscript about a fox family whose den was destroyed by the building of a subdivision.

"You know we live in the country, and the local wildlife rescue people told me about this fox family. A grader operator had found pups in the field he was grading. Luckily, they had been able to reunite them with the vixen who they found wandering in a nearby woods. Thought it would make a good story."

"Love it," Hollie said taking the manuscript. "I can see a dramatic drawing of the blade of the grader coming on the den and the pups scattering. Should be a film!"

"Okay, great. By the way, sorry to tell you that Grace has breast cancer and is in a bad way." Grace was Jonathan's wife. "It's been hard on me, too."

"I'm so sorry. What's the prognosis? Will she be okay?"

"Not great. It has spread. They did not catch it early enough. But we're hopeful."

"Well, let me know how it's going. I know the agony of having a partner with health issues." She reached out and took his hand. He had trouble looking at her.

"I'm bearing up, but I need to be busy…" They seemed to have little more to say. He was obviously going through a very rough patch.

"I should have some drawings for you in a week or so."

Hollie admitted she found Jonathan very attractive. Joe certainly liked him. But the poor guy. She knew they were a very loving couple who had not been able to have kids.

She worked hard at a few storyboards for the fox family yarn and a week later there he was at the door, looking worried.

"Are you okay?" she asked empathetically.

"Not really. Grace has a poor report on her cancer. It's spread a lot and a mastectomy won't get it all. But she'll have it anyway along with aggressive chemo which will leave her a wreck."

"Poor you!" She gave him an affectionate hug and kiss.

He liked the boards she had done and that cheered him up a bit. He left better than he had arrived. Hollie was taken with him and his sad situation. She had faced serious sickness and knew what he was going through, thinking the worst.

Another six weeks and the art was ready to be sent with the manuscript to the publisher. Hollie was pleased and so was the client. But Jonathan was clearly prepared for the worst, and sure enough a month later Hollie was sent the obituary for Grace Macintosh from Sammy. She felt so badly for Jonathan. She decided to write him a letter.

She found a plain elegant card with a painting of a sunset and wrote inside:

Dear Jonathan,

I know what you are going through. It is so tough and soul destroying to lose the one you love. But I believe they really don't leave you. Who they were for you stays with you in many ways. And I believe that love never dies. The one you love still inhabits the places she loved. So

> Grace may be gone but your love will live on. Mine does for Charles.
>
> Do let's get together when you feel up to it. I'm here for you.
>
> Affectionately,
> Your client and friend,
> Hollie

Jonathan opened this unusual personally addressed letter, pulled out the handwritten message and read it with growing emotion. Nobody had ever written such a warm, understanding, even loving letter to him—ever. He was in a fairly deep depression and in denial of the loss of his loved partner Here was a woman he knew was completely in sympathy with what he was going through. He was amazed.

He decided they would get together. He desperately needed a sensitive soul to talk to. Certainly, none of his golfing buddies could understand, since most of them really did not like their wives and constantly complained about them. Apparently, this was a manly thing that was beyond Jonathan's comprehension.

Hollie had almost forgotten her invitation to him when a month or so later he called, and they arranged to meet the following Saturday. Hollie decided she and Joe would go for a dog walk with him—it would be more relaxing than making conversation face to face.

So they did. It was a sweater wearing fall afternoon and after Joe gave Jonathan his friendly nuzzle, the three took the long walk down the street and around the corner to the woodlot entrance. Hollie could not resist telling Jonathan that this was where she had met Charles walking her dog many years ago, "A special place for me still," she admitted.

This warmed Jonathan up and he told Hollie about meeting Grace. He had known and dated her at college, but they had lost touch. She had a little niece who she doted on and one evening she was reading her a book which happened to be an early bunny story he had worked on with Hollie. She noticed his name on the cover and decided to find him, which she did with a roundabout email to the publisher, which eventually made its way to him. He replied, they had coffee, and "the rest is history," as he described it.

Hollie remembered Grace telling her at a party at her house about the coincidence that hers and her husband's book had a role in their getting together.

She decided, in typical Hollie fashion, it was time to let fate take its course and get to what was really on both their minds.

"It's been really tough for you?" Hollie took the lid off the black box they both shared.

"It sure has—a huge hole in my life, as I'm sure you know. I must say your letter was one of the few messages I got that showed any understanding, and a bit of hope."

"I was lucky I had Charles's daughter to cry with. And of course, my son. You don't have a lot of support?"

"Not really. I'm an only child and I don't think my mom really wanted me to marry. She isn't unhappy that I am more available now to see her."

"What about Grace's family?"

"She has an older sister and brother but wasn't terribly close to them. We didn't see much of them. Saw more of you and Charles in fact. It's only been six weeks or so and with her stuff she is still very much around in the house. And I'm having trouble writing."

"Well, Sammy laid down the law with me and told me eventually to get rid of all Charles's stuff. I even left his toothbrush in the bathroom for ever so long. We have to face up to the fact that our loved ones have gone, physically at least, but as I said I treasure dreams and other ways they are still available. Or at least their love is. It never dies."

By this time, they were down the path by the stream and stopped. They looked at each other. Jonathan was tall and had lots of almost orange hair framing a strong face, and big brown deep-set eyes. They were misty as he looked down and fixed on Hollie's bright blue eyes.

"That is so helpful and reassuring. You're wonderful."

He reached over and drew Hollie to him and they hugged.

"I suppose if Grace and Charles are watching, they wouldn't mind."

"I don't think so, and I have to say it's nice to be hugged by a man after all this time."

The walk ended and hey said goodbyes with a perfunctory kiss.

Thus began another slow love, a very slow love, but a love, nevertheless, between two sadder but wiser very grownup people. Always, in a strange way, under the watchful eyes of their late mates.

It turned out after much intense conversation that the relationships had been similar. Jonathan was a stay-at-home freelance writer, not just of children's books but of magazine articles and even vanity projects for a politician and a businessman who felt they had "books in them."

Grace was a high school teacher. Thy had moved to the country beyond the suburbs where she taught in a big suburban high school. They had a small house. No pets. But he had been brought up with dogs and Joe was all over him. Early on Hollie had told him, "Love me, love my dog."

Slow Love

"I don't think we are there are we?"

"No, but the only cure for loneliness which I know we both feel is to have a buddy, right? And it might as well be the opposite sex."

"We'll see," Jonathan was not ready, and they had only been seeing each other casually for a few weeks. But there was an attraction there and both knew it. They worked together on another book which brought them closer. A sequel to the fox story, which was selling successfully. Hollie found herself making editorial comments which he took easily. She had a good imagination for dramatic twists which the story lacked.

She had the vixen trapped by a farmer who hated foxes and taken to a nearby farm where it was put in an abandoned chicken coop. The male, called Rusty, tracked her and, in the night, dug and gnawed under the wire to free her. She made the rescue into a wonderful double spread drawing. Jonathan was tickled.

Perfunctory kisses were becoming a bit more affectionate, and one evening after working on the layout of the second fox book together, they had a beer on her couch squeezed together with Joe, and as usual Hollie took the lead.

"You know you are damned handsome and attractive. I would welcome a real kiss from you."

"I'm not against it," and he tentatively put his arm around her drew her to him and they locked lips.

"Wow, it' been so long. I forgot how nice a good kiss could be." Hollie was genuinely happy and felt a long-forgotten tingle move up her body.

"Grace was a good kisser. Was Charles?"

"Yes, even when he was older and got sick."

"Well, Grace always said that comparisons were odious. But what we just did was not enough to compare. Shall we?"

And they kissed more deeply, engaging their tongues. It was a revelation for both. They surprised each other and neither knew where to go from there.

"Given where we've come from with our two beloved late partners, do we dare sully their memories by falling in love again, if that's what's happening?" Jonathan was confused. Both were remembering their satisfying sex lives with their late partners.

"Have to ask what they would say if we asked them. Would they prevent us from finding new happiness? Or from being attracted to someone else? I wonder."

"I wish they'd give us a sign. I've had a few from Grace in dreams—mostly of the 'move on, but I still love you' variety."

"I've had those, too. But it was 'get back to work—life goes on.'"

"Well, gotta say you remind me of Grace. She was very much alive and energetic, and cared about me. But I think your creativity is what attracts me and sets you apart."

"Well, the more you share the more you care. Hey, I just made that up! But I am attracted to solid men. And that you are. Let's cool it for now and see how we develop. It would be nice to think of having someone caring to live with again."

"That's for sure."

"I guess good relationships are pretty basic. Two people who worry about each other and look after each other. That's what we both had and maybe we need it again. Physical love is a bonus."

"I agree. Maybe we should give it a try. Why not come up to my cottage with Charles's wonderful daughter and her husband, who you met here at a party some time ago. It's an important place for me, as it was for him."

"Hope he isn't there to disapprove."

"You never know!"

* * * * *

On Saturday morning the following week, Jonathan followed the complicated instructions and arrived down the back road in full autumn colour and honked at the top of the hill above the James cottage. Joe was up the hill to greet him, and he walked down the rough path with his bag and another one filled with bottles of wine along with a good bottle of gin and some tonic.

Hollie was at the door with a shawl over her red bathing suit and a big smile and a good kiss to welcome him.

"You are in the cabin down the path. Get your bathing suit on, we are on the dock. It's a bit cool but swimmable. See you at the dock."

He found himself thinking what a very lovely body this woman had. He hadn't seen much of it before. But her bathing suit left nothing to the imagination.

He looked down from his cabin with a bit of trepidation. Two teenage kids and her late husband's daughter and husband were draped about the dock lying out on it or on long lounge chairs. A standard poodle and Joe were stretched out in the shade up the path to the main house. He'd get a good looking over and he felt awfully untanned compared to them. He sailed a bit with friends on Lake Ontario but was not a cottage guy.

There he was, a tall white Scot in an old bathing suit, standing on the dock getting introduced.

"And that's our dog Willow on the path with Joe."

"Good to meet you all." He felt every one of them except Hollie scrutinizing him. Would he pass?

John, Sammy's husband, made it easy. He suggested a ride in the now old speed boat. Christopher and Julia wanted to come, and the dogs were not going to be left behind, either. Jonathan helped undo the lines and off they went.

"Well, he's big enough!" Sammy could not resist. Nor could Hollie.

"Don't know if he's big where it counts!"

"Come on, Hollie."

"No, we're taking it slow."

"I bet you're thinking about what my dad would say?"

"Yes, a bit. Being unfaithful to a strong memory is an issue I suppose I have."

"Well, I think you have to get over it. I can't believe he would not want you to be happy. So, are you happy with this big guy?"

"Well, yes. Not the same way as with Charles. He is tougher and not as sensitive. But I like him a lot and we've known each other for a long time and work very well together. And we both lost people we love. Same levels of sadness, I guess."

"I'm not sure yearning for the past is a good basis for a relationship," Sammy was finding this discussion somewhat odd.

"No, but we both share a feeling that our late mates are somehow part of us still. And we understand that in each other."

"Oh. So, are you physically attracted to him?" The two almost sisters could say almost anything to each other.

Hollie had to think about this answer.

"In a way he is more manly than Charles and I like that. Yet to be decided. We're not past hugging and deep kissing."

"I get it. Well good luck. He seems like a good type."

"Yes, he is. And Joe likes him."

"Well, I know that's important. Thank God. What about Christopher?"

"Hasn't really had a chance to get to know him. He's just met him in passing leaving the house after we've worked together. So, this weekend is the test."

Just then the big inboard boat swung into view and started to come up facing forward beside the dock for a landing. Jonathan was in the bow holding the bow line, ready to jump. At the last moment, the wind caught the bow, blowing the heavy craft away from the dock. Jonathan sprang up and took a huge leap to reach the dock—which he barely did, scrambling to his feet after a hard landing and pulling the bow in to the loud applause of the women on the dock. Hollie could see that her new guy's heroics made a good impression on Sammy on the dock and the rest in the boat.

Dinner prep time and time to change. The sleeping arrangements meant Hollie and Jonathan had to share

Slow Love

the sleeping cabin with its twin beds. Up they went, wondering about changing. Not a problem for Hollie who dropped her one-piece bathing suit quickly and grabbed panties, bra, and short shorts from the bed. Jonathan inadvertently got a peek at Hollie's firm body and small perfect breasts as he had modestly dropped his trunks under a towel and pulled up his boxer shorts. He felt a bit awkward and obviously Hollie did not. This was a very self-assured woman. They didn't say anything until Hollie, now dressed, said, "Enjoying yourself?"

"Yes, had a nice talk with your son. Seems like a good young man. We are both soccer fans."

"He is a good young man. I am lucky and he is very supportive of me."

"You're lucky. Teenagers can be difficult."

"Not mine—ready? It's drink time."

They walked over to the main cottage on the rough path.

Sammy was in the kitchen getting steaks ready for the BBQ and preparing vegetables, and husband John was out cleaning the big propane BBQ. Jonathan had carried from the cabin a good bottle of Tanqueray gin and some cans of tonic and as Hollie pitched in with vegetable prep, he offered to make drinks for everyone.

"Hey, it's still G and T weather. Can I make a good drink for everyone?" he announced loudly in his Scottish brogue. There was general agreement. Hollie showed him where everything was and he set to work. A lime was produced which he cut up. The result looked good on a tray which he passed around in the best waiter style.

He took his and the fourth drink out to John on the patio where he was firing up the BBQ.

* * * * *

"The kids get on well, it seems." Jonathan was curious about Christopher and Julia who were playing some card game in the cottage.

"Yes. They really grew up together. We saw a lot of Hollie and Charles and still see her and Christopher a lot. I warn you those two are a real pair. Very tight. I don't get away with a thing!"

Just then Sammy's loud voice rang out. "John, is the grill ready? Make sure it's really hot."

"Yes dear, give it a few more minutes. Just lit it." In a low aside to Jonathan, "See what I mean?"

"Well, it is rare that a daughter is so close to her stepmother. But they are so close in age I guess it was predictable."

"They are more like sisters for sure. They know each other's secrets and Sammy has been a huge confidante and support for Hollie through her dark time."

"Well, I am always amazed how close friends women can be compared to men. Hollie is lucky to have Sammy. I have noticed."

"So, to come back to your first question. Christopher and Julia were sort of bound to get on when their moms were so close. They are only two years apart and he is very protective and helps her with her studies and her technology. Looks after ours too."

Jonathan was starting to realize what a close, if unusual, family unit he was close to becoming involved in. It might be a challenge to be accepted, but he would work on it. He had not had anything like this with his late wife who came from a family that was not very close. And most of his relatives were still in Scotland, a brother and a bunch of cousins who he saw only on the occasional trip home to see his elderly mother who had died two years ago.

He soon got into the easy-going cottage life. Helping set the table in the cottage. Taking out the steaks, opening the wine, and chatting up the teenagers who were playing Euchre, a game he knew. He agreed to join them after supper.

The meal was marked by a discussion of a threatening development down the lake of a large island which featured a wonderful and rare sand beach that Charles used to take Christopher, Hollie and Julia to when the kids were learning to swim.

"I guess the beach will be off limits when they start putting in building lots," Hollie said. "But it's not over. The cottager's association has standing at a big hearing in the fall. And the island has a heritage designation."

"These are such unique and inviting lakes," Jonathan chipped in. "Not at all like our Lochs. And it seems like all sorts of people can enjoy them."

"Could enjoy them," Sammy interjected. "Good waterfront properties are hugely expensive now. Lucky us that Dad's father built this place after the war. I don't think either family could afford it now."

"Well, curiously I was checking prices for residences on Loch Lomond. They would all be around a million Canadian dollars. But having swum in both your lake and the Loch, the water is cleaner and warmer here. And as a guest in a big house on the Loch, it was pretty stiff—not here."

"Thank you, Jonathan. We try to make sure this place is informal." Hollie was happy that he was getting on and fitting in. He did play cards with the kids after supper, his offer to help with dishes being turned down. And there was lots of laughter.

After that he got into a discussion with Sammy and John about a magazine article he had done on the declining polar bear population which had taken him to the arctic. John collected Innuit art and had several large soapstone bears which were very precious to him.

Hollie was finishing up in the kitchen. Enough wine had flowed, and they all decided to turn in. The teenagers went out to the point to a large tent on a platform. Turning on the flashlight in her cell phone, Hollie led Jonathan to the little sleeping cabin.

"Hey, my friend, are you up for a naked swim?" Hollie couldn't resist. It was a bit of a test. She and Charles had often indulged and there was enough of a moon to illuminate the dock.

Caught off guard, Jonathan had to say yes. So, they grabbed towels in the cabin and went down to the dock.

Hollie peeled off her shorts, undid her bra and dropped her panties in a flash and stood briefly at the end of the dock ready to dive in. She turned around and teasing Jonathan who was eyeing her with some awe, called, "Come on, old guy, I'm ready. So long!" and she dove in.

He was not far behind and jumped in with a big splash. They swan out together.

"Pretty nice, eh?" Hollie said as they swam along.

"Indeed. A first for me. Not done in Scotland. Hope it isn't the last."

"Maybe not, but likely for this season. Our hot fall meant it stayed warm enough to swim this late. Another week or so of cold evenings and it won't be." She turned back towards the dock in a fast crawl.

She was up the ladder with a towel wrapped around her by the time Jonathan reached to ladder. She grabbed his towel and held it out as he climbed up. No full frontal, she thought.

They took their clothes and went up to the cabin where Hollie found her nightie and Jonathan his pajamas and put them on as discreetly as possible in the limited space. He could not help getting a short peek from the side of a perky breast.

Hollie slipped into one bed and as Jonathan was just about to slip into the other, she felt she had to show some affection and asked him,

"Do you want to kiss me goodnight? We are consenting adults and have kissed before!"

He had hoped something like this would happen but was not about to take the first step. He leaned over and kissed her on her ready lips. She pulled him down on her and let him have a second more passionate kiss.

"Hey, you are a good kisser! We can see if we want to take this further."

"I agree. We should go slow with all we've been through." He got up and slipped into his own bed. Warms good nights and sweet dreams were exchanged, and Hollie went to sleep thinking how Jonathan was heavier than Charles when he was on top of her.

Hollie woke up early, snoring coming from the bed opposite. She grabbed a towel, went down to the dock, slipped off her short nightgown and dove into the cool water. She got out, toweled herself dry, snuck back into the cabin, put on her shorts and top and went over to the cottage to get a pen and pad. She had had an amazing dream in which she knew she had communicated with Charles and wanted to write down what she remembered before it was lost. It was very important. This is what she wrote:

Charles made a ghostly appearance in my dream last night and to start with seemed to want to know how I was. He seemed upset about some unfinished business which I have read prevents ghosts from finding rest. It was obvious that he and I had not had a chance to say a proper goodbye. In some sort of way we accomplished that, with I love you's added. The exchange was not direct but more and exchange of things I felt and that I knew he understood. It was like a mind-to-mind contact session. I could not see him in my dream but felt his presence very strongly. He seemed to know I was okay but missed him terribly. He knew he had been my rock and partner in everything and my teammate. He let me know somehow about where he was. All in bright white, and now much better since we had a proper goodbye, however that worked. He was able to somehow see his parents. And he knew Grace, Jonathan's wife was in the same realm. I let him know I was seeing Jonathan and that we were at the cottage together. He seemed to know. I felt he had been around the cottage somehow, being sure that the dead never really leave the places they loved. Or those they loved. He was certainly present last night.

He let me know he was happy I was with Jonathan and that he was a good man. But he made it clear that our love would never die and that where he was love infused everything. Love was an eternal force that surrounded all the souls that were there. If Jonathan and I loved each other that was all that mattered. This is where the substance of the dream ended, and I recall simply rolling over as his presence continued to warm me and make me feel whole again for the first time in months.

Hollie put down the ball point pen and re-read it. Not very substantial for a visit from beyond the grave, she thought. But good advice for her and the big man sleeping in the cabin down the path. But the message was clear: be sure it is love, not loneliness or physical desire that was driving her into his arms. She had to be in his heart as well and he in hers. How was she to know? It was so evident with Charles after a few months and their time apart. She wondered whether Jonathan thought her happiness was more important than his own, a quality that endeared Charles to her. She also knew that love comes by grace, of its own will and in its own timing, subject to no human's planning. In that sense it had not come yet with Jonathan. Maybe it would—it needed time and shared experience. The weekend had been a good start. She decided he needed more Hollie testing.

Chapter Twelve

Charles had left Hollie with a sense of worry and care about the kids at the downtown social service agency where he worked over the years. The at-risk kids that nobody seemed to care about since some were bad kids and many were on the cusp of getting into drugs and gangs, one easy way for unloved young people to feel like somebodies.

Hollie remembered thinking when she first got a look at the youth program, *what could she do to help?* So, in the fall after Charles died, she arranged to set up a Saturday morning drawing class for fourteen- to eighteen-year-olds. It started slowly but by spring eight kids attended. Some showed promise and it was satisfying to provide them with a creative outlet they had never had. Some liked drawing animals from photos, others portraits of each other. Two hours went by quickly with Hollie showing them technique with her easy-to-use coloured pencils. She tried to inspire them with her own drawings, and Innuit sketches of spirit birds and bears. She attracted a mixture of black and brown boys and young women. She heard their sad stories and was seized again with what a privileged life she had led.

She told Jonathan about her charitable work that day when they were relaxing on the dock after lunch. She told him one kid had asked who had written the stories that went with her art, and she told them about Jonathan and his writing. One young woman felt she could write stories, and Hollie made a mental note.

"So why don't you come down one Saturday and talk to this girl. Maybe mentor her and anyone else who ins interested in writing? Gotta give back, you know!" Hollie wanted to challenge him and was surprised by the answer from the often-dour Scot.

"Funny you know I was thinking about that. I give to the United Way but have never done anything active for the disadvantaged. Likely because in the 'burbs they are invisible, or almost."

"You'll get a shock when you meet my kids and hear their stories. We do live in a bubble, you know."

"Might do me good. Sure, I'll come down. Next Saturday. Deal?"

"Great." He passed. She definitely liked him more and sent him a loving look which he returned.

Hollie looked around and took in her son and Julia, well-fed, well-clothed, well-educated. Leading lives most of her kids in her class could not even dream of. My work downtown keeps Charles's values alive inside me, she thought.

So, at 9:00 a.m. sharp the following Saturday he pulled up in his spotless older Volvo and a half dozen kids were waiting in the hall of the agency on a somewhat rundown side street off one of the city's main east-west corridors. Four trestle tables had been set up and drawing pads and pencil sets were at the ready.

"Hey artists," Hollie announced enthusiastically. "I have a surprise today. This is Jonathan, who wrote several of my books and does other writing well. Miranda," she addressed a thin black girl with pink pants and a profusion of long dreads. "I know you said you'd like to write a story. So why not sit with Jonathan in the lounge and talk to him about it?"

The girl got up and disappeared with the tall Scot. Hollie prayed it would work.

It did. On the way home a much different Jonathan told her all about it.

"Miranda's mom is from Ghana and her dad left them as soon as they came to Canada when she was five. So,

Slow Love

she had to work two jobs, mostly cleaning houses and offices to keep the family afloat. The real story is about her brother who is a couple of years older and got in with a bad group. Soon he was getting paid to hide drugs for a dealer. Then one day the dealer claimed that the stash he had given him was missing some hash and smacked him around. He was terrified and told the agency's youth worker about it. I think you have met Steve, the big black guy from the islands with dreadlocks," she nodded, "He told the lad in no uncertain terms he had to break off with the dealer right away and that he would look after him. Steve knew the dealer who hung around in the evenings off a busy corner in a big black Ford selling soft drugs to men and women from the rich neighborhood to the north of the poor east side district that the agency served. He knocked on the window.

'Hey man, you messed around with a young man recently for supposedly shorting you on a stash bag you gave him.'

'Yeah, so. He's gotta learn a lesson.'

'Well, I know the kid. He would not short you and he wants to get out of this racket and I want to make sure he does, and you leave him alone. Do you hear me?'

"And he grabbed the door and rocked the car. This made an impression. Story over and as Steve was fond of saying, 'Just have to show the kids that they can make a choice. And this kid made the right one.'

"Miranda told me that her brother, now seventeen, was learning hospitality skills at a small coffee shop and snack bar run by the agency and was a new kid.

"There are more gruesome details about the kind of life the family lives and the drug trade and how they use kids. All in all a good story that needs telling.

"I made notes but told her to write it out and we could maybe submit it for the agency's online blog. Changing the names, of course. She's going to email me a draft next week and I'll call her, and we can work it over. I'm pleased—she was all up and happy."

"Well. There. Are you glad you came to see the other side of me?"

"Yes, I'm impressed. It was just as you said. Time to give back for sure. Maybe we could set up a writing mentorship."

Hollie decided she liked him more. But not love yet. But the way he looked at her was changing. There was a warmth in his eyes that was not there before.

Well, Miranda did write a 1,000-word piece on her brother's experience and reform. Jonathan helped her with it and Hollie arranged for it to go on the agency's blog. The girl was thrilled, even though it was decided not to attach her name to it. All her friends knew, and she was very proud.

Jonathan thought it would be a nice idea to invite her for lunch downtown. "Bet she never goes out."

A week later, on a cold November morning they drove down to the old apartment complex where Miranda lived. She was waiting outside, wearing a flowered short dress and slick red ski jacket, her hair all done up and lots of red lipstick. She looked very pretty, and Hollie told her so as she got in the car. She was pleased.

They went to a well set up Mexican tapas bar not far from her house. They had a reservation and were taken to a small table. Miranda was confused by the number of small items on the menu and Hollie explained the tapas tradition of eating a larger number of smaller orders and sharing. She offered to order. Soon a large plate appeared with triple guacamole, which included a watermelon and plum version along with traditional; shrimp and chorizo street tacos; and the skirt steak tapas, a potted dish with a picadillo tang and cheesy topping; as described on the menu. They dug in enthusiastically.

Miranda did not take much encouragement to talk about school. She was in grade 11 and had no idea what to do with her life after.

"There's not much incentive to go on. We could not afford college and I don't think I have the marks. Most of the girls get a job, then a boyfriend, then it's over. Not much of a future."

"What if you pumped up your marks next year and I paid for college for you?"

Hollie was amazed at his offer and her face showed it. But proud too.

"Are you kidding? That would be awesome!" Miranda was a bit awestruck.

"Consider it done. But you'll have to be in touch next year and send me your marks. And decide where you want to go. There are good writing courses at community colleges. Or you could take social work and come back and help kids in this community. Check out the colleges and let me know what appeals."

"Okay. This is amazing. Maybe I'll have a future after all. Thank you so much." She was a bit embarrassed and looked down at her plate.

"Are you sure this is for real?"

"Yes. I don't have kids so haven't had to fork out for college. This is something I want to do, and I don't have to adopt you!" They smiled at each other. "I just want to follow your progress."

And he did. She emailed him with her mid-term marks, which did improve. They had lunch every few months. He became a bit of a father figure, obviously, and he felt close to her and found the experience life-changing.

Hollie noticed and they talked a lot about inequality of opportunity and how governments did not understand the challenges faced by the children of the poor. Miranda was certainly one. She had never had new clothes and shoes were always an issue. Hollie offered to bring some of hers down to her place since they had the same shoe size. She was thrilled. There was a pair of red low heels which she loved. And a barely worn pair of expensive runners. Jonathan told Hollie she was wearing them when he met her for lunch in January.

They decided to put aside the royalties from the fox books, which were selling well, to pay for Miranda's tuition the following year. It felt good.

One evening the phone rang and it was a sad little voice on the other end announcing herself to Hollie as Gabriel, Miranda's mom. She had a very soft accent.

"Hope I am not bothering you, but I wanted to thank you both for all you are doing for my daughter. You have given her hope and she is working hard. There is so little I can do. No money or time. I owe you a lot. You are the answer to a mother's dream." She sniffled.

"Come on. No problem. She is such a nice girl and ambitious now. She can probably have a good life now, and we are so happy to be able to help." She thought of her own Christopher with everything and Miranda with so little.

"Oh, and tell your friend that Miranda loves his accent."

It was a reassuring call for sure. Especially after a phone call from a woman on the Board who was an activist and found out about Jonathan's relationship with Miranda. When she got him on the phone she questioned its appropriateness.

"What are you saying?" Jonathan had asked. "Look, I have been mentoring her in a program approved by your youth worker. I went through your police check and sensitivity training. Is it wrong to want to give back? I admit I am a privileged white man. And lots of us support the agency in different ways. By the way, her mother is thrilled about the change that the possibility of going on in school has made in her daughter." He was forceful and that ended the conversation.

This whole experience had brought Hollie and her tall Scottish friend closer together. They were seeing a lot of each other, going to galleries and museums and even concerts. He was a good date and they talked easily and enjoyed the same experiences. Especially art, which pleased Hollie to no end. It was Charles all over again. As she was fond of saying, in a new version: "Sharing makes a pairing!"

One day she sat with Joe on the couch, and they had a chat about whether she should go the second mile with

Jonathan. He wagged at the mention of his name; he did like him, and Hollie took this for a positive sign. "Okay, old boy you may have another change in your life!"

He did. It was at Christmas with the family that after much discussion and trepidation they announced they would be engaged and live together. It had just happened one late cold November evening in Jonathan's country house, which was full of Grace memorabilia. He had blurted out, "You know I love you!" for the first time and she easily responded that she loved him too. They had had a good take-out chicken dinner and a bottle of white wine and were settled on his big couch. She was about to drive home but after their pledges of love he persuaded her to stay.

They both were ready, and she had to tell him that he was very heavy as they undressed in his large bedroom with huge windows overlooking a big, treed lot.

"I think it'd better if I was on top!" He had to agree and crawled into bed on his back while she straddled him and looked down on his big hairy chest and a big hardening penis which she grabbed enthusiastically.

"You're not shy, are you?" he asked rhetorically.

"Can't be, if you want to make love successfully," she admitted.

To their relief it was successful. And right after they decided to get engaged and to live together.

"I know our love will last," Hollie was confident.

"I know it will too." She rolled over and looked at the framed picture of a lovely Grace on the side table, with a lovely swish of dark hair half covering an eye. Sexy for sure.

"Sorry to ask, but am I better than Grace?" she asked.

"Different for sure, I'd say. But very good." She was aggressive compared to Grace and he liked it.

Slow love had turned fast, and it was good.

* * * * *

The second wedding for them both was a small family affair in March at Hollie's house after the basic city hall ceremony. Sammy and John made frozen hors d'oeuvres and the kids (Christopher now had a beautiful Sri Lankan girlfriend and Julia had a very athletic beau, both of whom were there) passed champagne. Steve came and made quite an impression as did Miranda. It felt right. Jay Godsoe, their publisher from Acorn books and his wife Charlotte were invited. They had become friends. And one connection with the past, Ashleigh, who was now running Charles's business, and her handsome husband Barrie. She was effusive about Hollie's new life and reminded her of how much she and the office still missed Charles. Seemed he was watching over them and

Slow Love

pleased. Unfortunately, both Hollie's parents were too old and weak to attend.

Willow and an old Joe were there but did not have a role like the two dogs did in Hollie's last wedding.

Moving in together was complicated as they decided to sell Jonathan's country place and set up shop in Hollie's, which had a bit more space and was handier to the city. He had a tough time leaving the house where he and Grace had a happy life. Too many memories, which he found himself sharing with Hollie as they packed and sorted years of stuff. He admitted he could not see himself shedding some things like the mahogany trestle table Grace had given him after a particularly rich ghost book assignment had come through. It would go in Hollie's living room which would be his office. Grace had much newer and better linen than Hollie, so it was kept as was his nice oak three-drawer bureau. Also, some of his kitchen appliances were more modern. All in all, the merger of the two households made for one very well-equipped house.

Hollie was glad to see that Jonathan had lots of garden stuff and alleged he was going to really work on her garden, which needed it.

The move in April saw a very enhanced Hollie home. They settled in easily and before long were working together on a new project. This time a story about a stowaway sparrow that had come to Montreal on a transatlantic cargo ship, and had become a bit of a pet of the crew. It made a new life among the big city sparrows in Montreal. Hollie had seen a news clipping about it and its release. It was an animal immigrant story, and it was coming along well. The sparrow from Manchester even had to learn new chirps to be understood. Hollie was finding it difficult to make expressions on the little bird's face but was working on it. Their publisher loved the idea.

Their philanthropic work at the agency was expanding with both art and writing mentoring going well. They were also raising money. They now had a room in the main headquarters they could use twice a week, Friday evenings and Saturday mornings. Jonathan had scrounged some old computers, and Hollie had easels. A couple of her pupils had gone on to art college and were doing illustration. She kept in touch with them. Jonathan's kids were doing a weekly community newspaper. The work was very important to both.

Hollie and Jonathan were the same age, and both turned 60 the same year. Their publisher Jay Godsoe who they saw quite a bit of was determined to throw a proper party at his club in late May.

It was a stuffy downtown club in an old mansion. Ties required. It was a fancy sit down dinner for twenty in a big alcove in their grand dining room. Jay used it for promotion and invited a couple of children's bookstore owners who Hollie and Jonathan knew from doing book signings in their stores. And the German-born agent he used for foreign sales, which had gone well over the years. Plus the family and the two kids—without their partners, on this occasion—who were now in their twenties.

Hollie and Jonathan were dressed to the nines and looking in the mirror decided they were a handsome couple: the tall Scot in a well-cut dark suit and red tie with his reddish hair and strong features, and Hollie with her long blonde hair up in a roll and a form-fitting short yellow dress and big silk shawl.

Jay was effusive. "Canada's children's book writing royalty," he declared, introducing the family as they all sat down and were served champagne by waiters with white gloves.

It was roast beef or fish, and the dinner went on with the booksellers anxious to know what was in the pipeline. Jonathan waxed on about *The Stowaway Sparrow* and all were charmed. Jay had a chart showing overall sales by books from Hollie and Jonathan and the total for both including overseas and US sales was over $100,000. There was applause. Hollie thought of Miranda's tuition which some of this was still paying for.

"No movie rights yet," he admitted. "But I'm working on it for the fox books."

Jay had a special edition of Hollie's first book *Bob the Bunny* in leather with a gold engraved title to give her as a gift. Hollie thanked everyone for coming and said with some emotion how the children's book business had brought her and Jonathan together as man and wife after they both lost their mates.

"I never thought of us as royalty, but we'll take it—won't we, Jonathan?" he nodded in agreement and there was applause.

* * * * *

Their actual birthdays were a month apart in June and July and they decided to have one party at the cottage with the family. Jonathan invited his older brother Jack from Scotland who arrived a couple of days early and stayed with them. He was also big and lusty and had a loud voice and booming laugh. He was very sociable, a retired professor and widower with a raft of grown kids. The brothers had not seen each other for ten years and had not been close but the reunion was warm with lots of tales of growing up together and boyhood pranks exchanged. He was a hugger and gave Hollie a lot of strong embraces with a "You're for sure a lovely one, Hollie! My brother doesn't deserve you!" accompanied with a hearty laugh.

The good humour continued at the cottage. The brothers were competitive and decided to have a swim race to the point across the bay and back. Sammy and Julia bet on Jack, and Hollie and Christopher bet on Jonathan. They churned over in a dead heat, but Jonathan had a better turn and came into the dock a bit ahead. They got their breath back sitting on the edge of the dock. Hollie embraced Jonathan, "My hero!" she shouted. The young people brought down a cooler of beer and all was well.

Since that Saturday, June 20 was actually Hollie's birthday and her husband's was two weeks later, the party was that night was for both of them. "Still Sexy at 60" was the theme of the party, invented by Sammy, and she had a very large poster made up with sparkles and ribbons, which was put on the mantel. "Something to live up to," she whispered to Jonathan as they came into the main house before dinner. "I don't feel challenged!" he replied.

Jonathan felt he had to give a toast to Hollie. It was easy:

"Let's raise a glass to Hollie, who looks about forty and I assure you at sixty is still sexy! I was so lucky that she came into my life when she did. And perhaps that goes for her too." He looked at Hollie and she nodded and blew him a kiss.

"We had both lost people we considered our life mates and were both in despair. We both lost our appetite and didn't get it back for several months. It was scary. But shortly after my Grace died, I got a note from Hollie which brought me to tears. She said love never died and that our lost partners would never really leave us. That kind of deep understanding is what brought us together." He wiped a tear from his eyes.

"We waited a long time as you know to decide to get together and stay together. I had to be tested by Hollie, up here for sure and in terms of what we shared in values and beliefs. Thank God I passed! Finally, we fell in love and exchanged love pledges. Sounds funny since it seems backwards. It's usually fall in love and then make sure we get on. For us it was make sure we get and on and then fall in love. I highly recommend it."

He looked at Christopher and Julia, who nodded.

"So Hollie, thanks for making our slow love work, and here we are and I'm part of this family. And I know Grace and Charles approve—right?" He tipped his glass up at the ceiling. "What, no lightning bolt?" Hollie exclaimed! And they all laughed.

"So, if I'm not mistaken **Sláinte** is the Gaelic toast—to you, darling Hollie!"

Jack, of course led the applause but shouted that Jonathan had mispronounced the toast badly and had to correct him.

"Thank the Lord we're not at home," he said. "Speaking of which, when are you going to bring your lovely wife over to meet her new family?"

"Soon, I hope." Jonathan realized that it was time to do just that.

Hollie was not about to be upstaged when it came to talking about love, which had been and was the motivating force in her life. She was prepared, of course, and had a love sonnet to recite. She had it folded in her bra and pulled it out, unfolded it dramatically and stood up.

"This sonnet is by Elizabeth Barrett Browning and sums up the love I had for Charles and I now have for my darling Jonathan:

> How do I love thee? Let me count the ways.
> I love thee to the depth and breadth and height
> My soul can reach, when feeling out of sight
> For the ends of being and ideal grace.
> I love thee to the level of every day's
> Most quiet need, by sun and candle-light.
> I love thee freely, as men strive for right.
> I love thee purely, as they turn from praise.
> I love thee with the passion put to use
> In my old griefs, and with my childhood's faith.
> I love thee with a love I seemed to lose
> With my lost saints. I love thee with the breath,
> Smiles, tears, of all my life; and, if God choose,
> I shall but love thee better after death.

"There, if I die tomorrow you can put this in my grave where love will never end. Thanks."

Jack left a week after the party. Hollie realized how reassuring it was for Jonathan to see one of his family when it was hers that dominated in the household.

Chapter Thirteen

The summer and fall and cottage weekends right through the glorious rich autumn colours followed. The reds were particularly spectacular—almost day glow red on some maples on the drive in. They were both busy on new assignments: Hollie had a new children's book about climate change and a young girl, modelled loosely on Greta Thunberg, who took up the cause at the school. Of course, she had a dog called Mutt who was a constant companion and often stole the show with his vocalizing.

Jonathan had another ghost book which was driving him crazy. The PR people at one of the major banks had decided to have a book written and published about the retiring chairman's life and it was difficult to make a readable work out of a bank lifer whose sole outside interest was his collection of sports cars. Jonathan was allowed a strict maximum of twenty hours of the man's precious time at his mansion in the evening for interviews. He did get to look at the three Jaguars, an Austin Healey and a rare Lamborghini. And it was money, good money. Vanity writing was a good gig, if creatively unrewarding.

Meanwhile Hollie had picked up a very old used book she had bought years ago by Ernest Thompson Seton: *Wild Animals I Have Known*. She had bought it hoping for good animal drawings, but alas there were only poor etchings of various beasts. However, she did get into the first story, Lobo the King of Currumpaw. It moved her more than she could imagine. She gave Jonathan an edited version of this wolf story from the late 19th century. It had become very famous:

> Lobo was a North American gray wolf who lived in the Currumpaw Valley in New Mexico. During the 1890s, Lobo and his pack, having been deprived of their natural prey such as bison, elk, and pronghorn by settlers, became forced to prey on the settlers' livestock to survive. The ranchers tried to kill Lobo and his pack by poisoning animal carcasses, but the wolves removed the poisoned pieces and threw them aside, eating the rest. They tried to kill the wolves with traps

and by hunting parties but these efforts also failed.

Ernest Thompson Seton was tempted by the challenge and the $1000 bounty for the head of Lobo, the leader of the pack. Seton tried poisoning five baits, carefully covering traces of human scent, and setting them out in Lobo's territory. The following day all the baits were gone, and Seton assumed Lobo would be dead. Later, however, he found the five baits all in a pile covered by wolf feces to show Lobo's contempt and mockery of Seton's attempt to kill him and the other wolves.

Seton bought new, specialized traps and carefully concealed them in Lobo's territory, but he later found Lobo's tracks leading from trap to trap, exposing each. When an effort that was initially supposed to take two weeks stretched into four months of failed attempts to capture Lobo, Seton became tired and frustrated. While camping out he found Lobo's track strangely following a set of smaller tracks. He realized Lobo's weakness: his mate, a white wolf nicknamed Blanca.

Seton then set out several traps in a narrow passage thinking Blanca would fall for Seton's planted baits that Lobo had thus far managed to avoid. Finally Seton succeeded; Blanca, while trying to investigate Seton's planted cattle head, became trapped. When Seton found her, she was whining with Lobo by her side. Lobo ran to a safe distance and watched as Seton and his partner killed Blanca and tied her to their horses. Seton heard the howls of Lobo for two days afterward. Lobo's calls were described by Seton as having "an unmistakable note of sorrow in it... It was no longer the loud, defiant howl, but a long, plaintive wail." Although Seton felt remorse for the grieving wolf, he decided to continue his plan to capture Lobo.

Despite the danger, Lobo followed Blanca's scent to Seton's ranch house where they had taken the body. After spotting Lobo wandering near his ranch house, Seton set more traps, using Blanca's body to scent them. Prior to this point, Lobo hasn't revealed himself to Seton even once since he arrived at the

Slow Love

Currumpaw Valley. But now Lobo's grief has clearly taken over him and dulled his sense of caution. He was now at his most vulnerable, which Seton was well aware of. On January 31, 1894, Lobo was caught, with each of his four legs clutched in a trap. On Seton's approach, Lobo stood despite his injuries, and howled. Touched by Lobo's bravery and loyalty to his mate, Seton could not kill him. He and his men roped Lobo, muzzled him and secured him to a horse, taking him back to the ranch. Lobo refused to eat or even look at his captors. They secured him with a chain and he just gazed across his fallen kingdom. Lobo died that night, four hours later, due to a broken heart.

Until his death in 1946, Seton championed the wolf—an animal that had always previously been demonized. "Ever since Lobo," Seton later wrote, "my sincerest wish has been to impress upon people that each of our native wild creatures is in itself a precious heritage that we have no right to destroy or put beyond the reach of our children."

Hollie also shared her research which told of Seton's story of Lobo touching the hearts of many, both in the US and the rest of the world and being partly responsible for changing views towards the environment. It apparently provided a spur for launching the conservationist movement. The story also, she discovered, had a profound influence on one of the world's most acclaimed broadcasters and naturalists, Sir David Attenborough, and inspired the 1962 Disney film, *The Legend of Lobo*. Lobo's story was also the subject of a 2007 BBC documentary.

"Impressive," Jonathan agreed as they sat down that evening to discuss the story. "Have you an idea for us to do a similar yarn?"

"Precisely—an illustrated book for all ages with a similar dramatic ending showing this animal's undying love for its mate. Something we do know a lot about. Yes?"

"Where would it be set though?"

"Obviously, our wolves would have a pack in Algonquin Park. I know they used to have public wolf howls in the fall that were very popular. There must be lots of wolves there. I'm going to do some research, and you can think of a story line."

"I can see its appeal. Almost Disneyesque. But we have to be authentic and avoid cuteness."

They agreed and Hollie started to research. She got in touch with the park and discovered David, an experienced naturalist who sent her articles in the park publication on wolf research that had been going on for years. She discovered that the couple behind the most extensive ten-year long field research were John and Mary Theberge who had written a book called *Wolf Country: Eleven Years Tracking the Algonquin Wolves*. She ordered a used copy as it was out of print. She devoured it even if much of it was technical since it was the story of tracking radio-collared wolves on the ground or from light planes. It had good photos and many stories of actual sightings. She also bought an amazing National Geographic book *The Hidden Life of Wolves* by filmmakers Jim and Jamie Butcher, which was the well-illustrated story of their adoption of pups and raising a pack in a large, enclosed area in Idaho. The photos were extraordinary, including excellent images of wolf language, how they communicate with each other and show their status in the pack through posture, facial expression, tail and body position. These insights would be critical for Hollie's illustrations. Unfortunately, these shots were of grey wolves and the Algonquin wolf was smaller and had different coloring, shown in the Theberge book and the park publications. The Algonquin wolf was an Eastern wolf with tawny orangey brown on their snouts and legs, mixed with dark fur on their back and often white around their muzzles—more appealing and individual than grey wolves, Hollie thought.

To her delight she found a Theberge story that confirmed the Lobo drama. He had found out from a man who had killed a radio-collared dominant female with pups outside the park. He went outside and found the other radio-collared wolf who was emitting a distinctive and very moving mourning howl. Other researchers have heard this howl when deaths of pack members have occurred. She was also very encouraged by a passage in another large book on wolf research which concluded that wolves have emotional lives as rich and complicated as our own. This would give Jonathan permission to inject emotions into the story of their wolves. And years of research and observation has proven what natives believed, that wolves are all individuals. Wolf societies, like human societies, consist of different personalities, from mean bullies to caring compassionate helpers, from playful and sociable animals to the lonely and stand-offish. From the bonded alpha male and female who were pack leaders and alone could reproduce, to the omega wolf that everyone picked on. This variety of characters would feed the couple's creativity. Hollie shared all this with Jonathan who was considering the story and its wolf personalities.

Hollie did peruse the most infamous Canadian book about wolves, Farley Mowat's amusing 1963 book *Never Cry Wolf*, about a wolf family in the far north. It was considered fanciful by critics but did lead to re-evaluation of the alleged role of wolves in decimating caribou herds. She did like one of his quotes though: "Wolves are strict monogamists, and although I do not necessarily consider this an admirable trait, it does make the reputation for unbridled promiscuity which we have bestowed on the wolf somewhat hypocritical."

So, a devoted monogamous pair of defined wolf characters and their family and relatives in a close-knit pack. That was what they would work with.

But Hollie was beginning to feel a real yearning to go to Algonquin and to try and experience wolf life there firsthand. She had been told that late winter was best, since finding tracks was easier and kills on lakes were easier to view. She was secretly dreaming of looking a wolf in the eye and experiencing the Indian saying she had read in several wolf books: "to look into the eyes of a wolf is to see your own soul." And as an artist she was fascinated by the fact that wolf eyes were golden yellow.

"Why would you want to go into the wilds and camp in winter?" Jonathan was very skeptical about the idea and did not see what it could contribute to their project.

"Well, I think our story should be set partly at least in winter. That is when our pair will mate, have pups three months later and when their hunting is easiest. I want to get a feel for the landscape for my illustrations, and maybe I'll see some wolves. It's possible, I'm told."

"Who will you go with? I have no desire to sleep in the snow."

"Well, I'll have to find someone who knows the territory and wolves—I'm working on it."

And she was. She googled the names of photographers who were credited with wolf photos in the park's publications David had sent her. She lucked out with the second, one David Robertson, a wildlife photographer. She called him and as it turned out he was planning a four- or five-day winter trip to the western park that year in March. She explained her project and he seemed open to her accompanying him. They checked each other out and talked again. Hollie liked the fact he was married with two kids and lived in the country south of Collingwood. He had been to the park often to photograph wolves and had learned how to howl convincingly. She knew that the Theberges had used their howling regularly to locate wolves. It worked.

Jonathan became inured to the fact that his love would be camping with another man—a younger one at that. He trusted her and was happy that David would rent a satellite phone.

So, March 15 finally came. They were going to meet at noon at the liquor store in Kearney, a small-town east of Elmsdale on Highway 11 north of Huntsville. Their cottage was south of Huntsville and Hollie estimated the time correctly, leaving at 9:00 a.m. and arriving at the small outlet at 11:45 a.m.

Five minutes later a big green Jeep Cherokee rolled up, and out came a well-built bearded man in yellow snow pants, huge white canvas boots and a big blue parka, David Robertson for sure. Hollie got out of her Toyota Camry and they formally greeted each other.

"So, you're Hollie," he said with a hearty grin. "Glad to meet ya. Since we're here, might as well get a dram of whisky to keep us warm. Any preference?"

Hollie liked his approach and the twinkle in his eye. "No, but I like Johnny Walker."

"Good choice and comes in a small bottle."

After purchasing the bottle, they decided to have lunch in the small family restaurant up the main street. Over burgers and fries they exchanged the normal basic information about their lives. Her parka off, Hollie noticed she was being looked over by David who seemed pleased with what he saw—he was. David was from Parry Sound, a true northerner, and had married his high school sweetheart. He was fifty-five and took up photography after getting tired of teaching high school in Collingswood. While wedding and school gigs kept bread on the table, his real love was nature photography and a chance sighting of a wolf on a camping trip with his family had hooked him on the animal. He had attached himself to government researchers on a couple of summers in 2005 and 2006 when there was a lot of radio collaring going on, and complied a fairly extensive collection of photos including a lucky few shots of pups. But he hadn't done anything in winter and badly wanted to get photos of a kill.

He was impressed by Hollie's research about wolves. He checked out the equipment she had brought and seemed satisfied. He had more equipment than fit in his pack. Luckily, she had room in hers for pots and other cooking gear. They would repack at the ranger cabin just inside the park where David had arranged for them to stay the first night.

They set out for the hour-long drive east down the ever-narrowing snow-covered road to its end a few hundred yards from Rain Lake and the ranger cabin. They parked, heaved up their backpacks, strapped on their snowshoes and set out. The small log cabin hove into view overlooking the frozen lake. David had the key and stepping into the cabin it was clear it was well equipped with a propane stove, fridge and two hanging lights. An old chesterfield looked out through big windows over a screened veranda above the lake. There was a simple board table and straight back chairs. Hollie was relieved that there were two small bedrooms.

"You take the one on the lake side," Jonathan said. It had a small window looking over the lake. Hollie took in her backpack and took out her new sleeping bag. It was a simple old fashioned metal spring bed with a thin mattress. Better than the ground, she thought.

David busied himself unpacking food for dinner and checking the appliances. He put some frozen food outside in a closed wooden box on the side of the house that had a hasp with a stick through it.

"Let's go outside and do a few howls and see if there are any wolves around," he said. Too good, Hollie thought.

An obvious path wound down and crossed a frozen stream to the other side of the lake. They walked along the lakeshore for a few a hundred yards. Hollie had no trouble keeping up with David. He turned and asked, inappropriately he knew, "How old are you? I know it's bad form, but you are obviously fit."

"I'm sixty one," she said without hesitation. She knew the answer.

"Well, I really find that amazing…you sure don't look or act that age."

"Thanks," she said. "I work on it." She was used to this exchange and liked it a lot.

After about twenty minutes of snowshoeing up the lake, David cupped his hands and let out a series of mounting and very convincing howls.

As Hollie clapped her big ski mitts in admiration, they could hear a distant low then mounting howl joined by at least two others in a short chorus. The howls came from up the narrow top of the lake to the northeast.

"Are we lucky or what?" David exclaimed. "They might even be celebrating at a kill up the lake." Their howling continued as they went back to the cabin in the failing light. David was sure that the low powerful howl was from an alpha male.

David had pork and beans and toast over the stove going in no time and they ate on their metal plates. They had two big plastic pails of snow melting and heated up water for washing the plates and the metal cups they used to toast their arrival in the park with a small whiskey. There was enough warm water for them to wash their faces. They poked their heads outside and listened in the cold stillness. More howls. Eerie but promising.

Hollie wanted to make her "love call" to Jonathan and asked Robert if she could briefly use the satellite phone. He was agreeable and thought it a good idea to phone home as well. The calls were a surprise and a success.

Next morning, they had porridge with powdered milk and coffee, divided the packs, repacked and headed out before 8:00 a.m. About four kilometres up the path, they noticed wolf tracks crossing it. They headed across the lake which had widened at this point. Hollie saw how big the paw prints were compared to those of her chocolate lab. She took her camera out from under her parka and took a few shots of the first sign that she was finally in wolf country.

They went up the path along the east side of the lake until it widened and paused at the first campsite marked on the map which looked across the widest part of the lake. Robert howled and got a response that seemed to come across the lake. There were wolves nearby.

They decided to set up cameras to see if they could make out anything the kilometer or so at the other shore. They struggled up the steep rocky hill overlooking the lake, took their cameras out from their parkas, and got out their longest lenses. Hollie discovered that her 300 mm was no match for David's huge 800 mm job. They put their cameras on tripods and searched out the other shore.

Sure enough, there was a kill and evidence of several spots surrounding it where wolves were apparently resting after their meal. Finally, one large one stretched and got up. He was clearly visible even to Hollie.

"I've got him almost full frame," David was exultant. "I think he's on the move. He is going to the kill and pulling off some meat."

Hollie could see him clearly too as he moved off and started to cross the lake towards them. David was sure he couldn't scent them as the wind was blowing towards them.

"I'll bet he's taking a meal for his mate back at the den. It's puppy time and they are still not weaned. Must be the alpha male."

They were so lucky and privileged to get such a good view of this shy creature, Hollie thought, and as he came closer, trotting purposefully, she saw how really special he was.

He was white around his jaw and his pricked-up ears were lined white. He was greyish white and black on his upper body and tan and white lower down and on his legs. He was smaller than she had anticipated, hard to tell, but he was well built. Not the slightest bit scrawny. It must have been a good winter. She knew that there were fewer deer in the western part of the park where they were, and the packs survived more on beaver and rabbits. But they did have a deer across the lake, and that would probably last the pack a few days. There were three other pack members stretching and getting up for another feed. They scared off the ravens who were already picking at the carcass. Hollie and David both clicked away. By this time the big male had disappeared into the bush further up the lake.

"Not much more that we haven't already got," David announced. "Let's move on. The next campsite is about five k's."

It was an overcast day but not too cold. The snowshoeing was easy since there'd been a thaw and the snow was only a foot or so deep. The path cut east at the end of the lake and crossed a frozen narrow inlet then followed an old rail line and crossed a wider inlet of the next lake, Inlet Lake, on the remains of an old trestle. The storied lumber past of the park. The campsite was on a bay of a tiny body of frozen water, Ishaday Lake. There were wolf tracks on the lake. It was now after three and they decided to set up camp and have a late lunch/early dinner. Hollie was nervous. David had done this before. She had not.

"Tents first, then wood for a fire." David declared, clearing out what looked like the fire pit.

She fumbled in her pack and out came the tent and its aluminum stays. She had practiced at home, but it was complicated. She spread the tent out on the snow and threaded the stays. The dome miraculously appeared and lifted into shape, and she put it on a flat space away from the fire pit and pegged the corners in the crisp snow. In went her pack—she was ready to forage for wood. Nearby pines had low branches that were dead and there was a big log in the woods with dead branches sticking up. Before long she had an arm full and proudly took it to David who had put up his tent and was returning with his own bundle from the other side of the campsite.

They smiled at each other. "Should do us for tonight," he allowed.

They both needed something warm, and Hollie got the pots and they melted snow on the propane burner and made powdered potato soup and ate power bars and some cheddar cheese.

Hollie wanted to compare their wolf photos and out came the cameras. They both had pretty good shots of the male. Hollie decided she'd call him Tristan the wolf and that he would be her principal character in her book. Isolde would be the alpha female. The story was already taking shape in her mind. She was delighted about the complex coloring of this unique species, the Algonquin wolf.

David was pleased too—with his huge zoom he had almost close-ups of the wolf.

Sitting on the big log David had cleared off at the fire pit, they launched into a discussion of marriage. They did not know how it came up, but it did.

"So how did you meet your wife?" Hollie was always curious about relationships.

"At Parry Sound High School, the biggest in the north. Over 600 students at that time from all over. She was the cute blonde that everyone wanted to date, and I was the shy student. But I lucked out. We skied at Hidden Valley in Huntsville, about a forty-minute drive from Parry Sound.

"I know it," Holly chimed in. "Our cottage is south of Huntsville. We shop there. So, you sealed the deal on the slopes?"

"Not quite, but it helped. I liked skiing, went with my parents, then on my own after I got my license. It was then we really met up, on the lift, believe it or not. We got talking and after skiing together spent the rest of many afternoons getting to know each other. I wasn't the shy studious guy anymore but a skiing buddy of this great looking girl, Shelah Falwell—and before you asked, no she fell very seldom!"

They both laughed. "How long before you got serious?"

David was not used to this charming line of questioning, but saw no reason not to share with this very sympathetic woman.

"Well. We were both just about to graduate and like in the movies were about to go to different universities. I was going to teacher's college in Toronto, and she wanted to go to Western and take journalism. So we had a tough summer—I was working at the Bayside Inn as a night front desk guy and she was waiting tables at the Brunswick

Sports Grill and Bar. Not ideal jobs for dating for sure. But we did manage the odd weekend afternoon at the beach before her 6:00 p.m. shift. Gotta say she was great in her bikini and we did a lot of necking as we used to say. But it would be a long time before we became intimate." The big guy paused. "I don't know why I'm telling you all this."

"Maybe because I'm an older, more understanding woman," she said with a twinkle. "Anyhow, I believe in slow love. That is what I had with my first husband—took us a long time to commit. And, by the way, we met over dogs not skiing."

"Well, she came a few times and visited me in Toronto. I had a crummy downstairs flat in an old house, and that is where things got serious. We'd both gone out with a few other people, but nobody came close to the kind of understanding we had with each other."

"Funny about relationships—they do grow, especially when you have others to compare with the ONE. I had to move in with another loser to find out what a gem my Charles was, even if he was much older."

"We got engaged while we were both in university. Then I took a job at Collingwood Collegiate Institute and Shelah found a reporting job at the Collingwood Enterprise Bulletin. It was a going concern but closed a few years ago. She worked there until Blue Mountain

Resort hired her away to do publicity. She still does all their PR and advertising."

"My first husband Charles had a PR agency in Toronto. James Public Relations. Became very successful."

"You say first husband—what happened to Charles?"

"He died nearly ten years ago of a heart attack... I'll never get over it."

"We lost a child, a boy in an auto accident. Run down on his bike by a drunk guy. I know what you mean. But the love you have for another person, whether a child or a mate never dies, does it?"

"No, that's for sure. That's one of the reasons I want to do a story about the devotion wolf couples have for each other and for the pack. It's extraordinary."

She told him about Lobo, and what the Theberges had said about wolves mourning the death of their mates. He listened intently.

It was now dark and time to make dinner. It would be pasta with dried spaghetti sauce and a little package of frozen ground beef. Two pots and a fire would make it easier, so David built one and fished out a rusty grill from near the pit. Lots of snow in the pots. It took a lot to get a couple of quarts and enough in the small pot to make the sauce, plus the meat in the little fry pan. Hollie was in charge of the meat and got out the one large metal spoon and David found a small plastic bottle of oil.

It was a happy meal which finally came together with a minimum of fuss. More snow and water for cleaning up and with a bit of dark chocolate for dessert they were ready to turn in. Not before David did a few wonderful howls in the very still very dark night that did get a return from much further east.

"Hear that low throaty first howl followed by a bit of a chorus?" he asked. "I'm sure that was our big alpha wolf. They are probably at the den. New pups are a big cause for singing and celebration."

They packed up after breakfast and set out the nine-kilometer path to a campsite on Gervais Lake. It wound south passing the large Brown Lake and a major wetland and beaver pond. They knew that beaver made up part of the wolf diet and that by March the industrious animal might be running low on twigs and emerge and be vulnerable to wolf predation. Twice lucky on a kill?

There were wolf tracks, likely old, on Brown Lake but no sign of the pack. David's howls in the morning got no reply. But as they closed on the low frozen marsh after a quick lunch of energy bars and chocolate and could make out the beaver pond to the north, suddenly there were closer answering howls.

They cut out and crossed to the large low-lying beaver pond and trudged through the dead trees seeing nothing. The pond widened out and, in the distance, they could make out the beaver house, its round snow covered shape sticking out near the shore. Beside it was what looked like a large spot on the lake and there was some movement around it, and a couple of ravens circling overhead. Wolves at a beaver kill, David was sure. He howled and got a nearby answer. But they were more than 500 yards away and couldn't really make much out. There was no cover, and they might scare the wolves away, so they got up on a small point of land on the shore that still gave them a view of the beaver house poking above the ice on the lake. There was a large snow-covered bush and they squatted behind it and set up their cameras and long lenses.

"It's our pack," David said triumphantly, squinting through his giant lens. "Can you make them out?"

"Not too badly," Hollie replied. "Our big male is pretty obvious, and two others seems to be hovering about."

"They are the adolescents waiting for permission to eat," David said. "The leader eats first."

They clicked away and watched for a half-hour. Suddenly the wolves must have got their scent and disappeared in the bush at the shore. The ravens descended to get their share.

Happy, they packed up and trudged back to the path. There was a campsite about three kilometers away and they wanted to make it. It was a sunny day but colder. They moved though pines and cedars, along the small

Gervais Lake then up and down two fairly high rocky hills to Tern Lake. It was tough going but the hard work kept them warm. It was a big campsite. The breaking of camp was now a routine and as the light faded, they were settled, a good fire was going and David was ready to cook. It was ravioli tonight with powered sauce and there was still some frozen ground beef for Hollie to cook on the fire. Their hands got cold eating, so they moved very close to the fire.

They talked about their kids that night. Christopher was still at university and unsure what to do with his life. He was still seeing his exotic Sri Lankan girlfriend.

David had two kids who he obviously doted on, an eighteen-year-old girl and fourteen-year-old boy. Gayle was, he admitted, very beautiful and the apple of his eye. He admitted that after she turned eighteen he invited her to the local pub, Flynn's Irish Pub in Collingwood, and thoroughly enjoyed the stares he got from patrons assuming she was the young date of this middle-aged man. They had a good laugh about this on the trip back. Hollie had a similar scene with Christopher at a local Italian restaurant she had invited him to on a weekend visit from Toronto.

"I'm sure some of the patrons thought I was out with my boy toy," she laughed.

Before turning in, David did a few howls and surprisingly got a single low throated reply that seemed close by. They agreed it must be the big male. Had he followed them? A few minutes later they heard crunching of brush up the hill behind them. David got out his big flashlight and turned it in that direction. It caught the glowing yellow eyes of the big male watching them from ten yards away. Hollie held her breath. She was actually looking into the eyes of a wolf. They stayed very still and with the flashlight off they could just make out the shape of the big male in the firelight. He turned and disappeared like a ghost. No time to get a camera out. But the image would be etched in their minds forever, they agreed.

Her little dome tent seemed very cold that night and she kept her snow pants on and crawled into her sleeping bag. She dreamt of the male wolf. What was he thinking, visiting their campsite? Was it just curiosity? Wondering if it was another wolf howling? He was not the least aggressive.

They had certainly been lucky—two kills and a visit. Lots of good shots. It was a long twelve kilometers in the sun the next day and a very high promontory ascend and descend. The top was marked as a lookout on the map and they stopped and had some soup overlooking the snowy forest stretching out below. Then the trail took them north along Wood Lake then Islet Lake to a campsite near the abandoned railway trestle they had crossed before. They saw some wolf tracks on the lake just before they made camp in a little sheltered bay. They decided it could have bene the same pack heading to the den site after gorging on the kill on adjoining Rain Lake. David's regular howling went unanswered.

"I think we've seen all we are going to," he said sadly. "Oh well, can't complain. I was crazy to think we would see their den site. Anyhow, they apparently have been known to move pups if they detect humans nearby."

"I'm not complaining, " Hollie said. "It's been a-mazing!" she said with as much emphasis as she could muster. She was tired. A long day of slugging on snowshoes.

They were quieter that evening. Their last supper and David had saved two small fillets. Hollie did powdered mashed potatoes, they had the last of the whiskey and it became quite festive. Thy admitted that they liked each other—after a typical Hollie intervention—and promised to stay in touch. Hollie invited David and family to the cottage that summer and he accepted, though he doubted Gayle would come.

"Going to the pub with dad is okay, but going away for a weekend with her brother? I doubt it."

"Never know, she and Christopher might like each other."

They both had a satellite "love call," Hollie gushing about what she had seen and experienced and Jonathan relieved they were both in one piece. They turned in.

They had nine kilometers the next day to get back to the ranger's cabin and their cars. They passed the place where they had seen the kill on the other side of the lake. Nothing left. David's howls still unanswered.

They said hello to an attractive couple in the cabin and they exchanged information on the loop they had made. They accepted the offer of a large pot of warm water on the propane stove to wash up. Hollie was very happy to be somewhat clean. And even happier to use the outhouse in back.

They repacked, David taking back the camping cooking gear, and said goodbye to the couple.

They were losing light and left to make the 100 yards or so to the parking lot. Both cars started. They hugged. It had been an adventure and they had genuinely liked each other.

"What did we used to say," David said as they looked at each other closely. "It's been real. Can't wait to see the book."

"It has, for sure. You'll get a copy as soon as it's out. That will be the fall, hopefully. But we'll see you before then."

She blew him a kiss and they left. Hollie was home by eight-thirty, stopping for a burger in Huntsville on the way.

Arriving home, she fell into Jonathan's arms after mad Joe lickings and greetings, then right into a hot bath. Oh, the luxury. Clean again finally. Her pile of clothes on the floor did smell and went right into the machine. Then they stayed up late for Hollie's somewhat exaggerated account of the wolf adventure.

"I've sketched out a plot and we can go over it tomorrow. So glad you're back." Jonathan had been lonely. And they went to bed and made love.

The next day they met in the living room with notebooks in hand.

"I think the wolf hero of our book has to be the big male I saw three times in Algonquin, and that my story of my wolf discovery, however incomplete, should somehow be part of the book. Would make it more real and human." Hollie was certain of this, Jonathan knew.

"Okay, how about a nice foreword about how you met…are we still going to call him Will?"

"No, I thought of Tristan and Isolde as names for the pair. It suits in every way," she said, and Jonathan continued.

"The story could begin with a chapter on Tristan and Isolde mating and having puppies in the winter. The first pups grow and the pack forms with a couple of other adopted adolescents. Then we do a flashback into how the younger Tristan leaves his pack in the east of the park as a dispersed wolf, as they call them, and seeks a mate in the western part where you were. There he meets Isolde, and they mate. Then the second litter over the next two years becomes the pack you saw. What do we call it?"

"Near as we can tell the den would have been near the next lake over Brule lake. So, we could call them the Brule Lake pack."

"Cool," Jonathan liked the sound of that. "Then we describe their devotion to each other and the devotion of the other members of the pack to the pups in the second litter. There can be an Auntie who watches them while they are out hunting. Oh, and by the way I thought perhaps Isolde could have left her pack because she was sick of babysitting –works, eh?"

"I like it. Good backstory for our couple." Hollie now understood what work Jonathan had put into studying wolf behaviour. "I think Tristan should find the photographers, like David and I, as part of the story, curious about the ability of the man to howl. Then the campfire scene where they stare at each other. It was such a defining moment for me."

"I like that and of course it is going to be humans who provide the tragic end to our story. But there have to be other incidents."

"Well, we know many pups die. We can have a bear take a pup. It does happen. And the sadness that overtakes the pack when this happens. Joy and singing at kills, sadness and a mournful howling at a loss."

"Okay," Jonathan made a note. "The pack has to venture outside the park for the ending to work. So that could be a story line in a lean winter with stories of unsuccessful deer chases. No beaver. Living on the odd rabbit. A pup dies of starvation. They had to go far beyond the park to hunt, past the protected areas. Then we must invent a trapper who discovers there's a new pack in his rural area and sets snares. And of course, Isolde gets snared and she and Tristan have a sort of libestod or love-death scene before the trapper comes, then he stays near and mourns her, then follows her body flung on the trapper's ATV to his house. He won't leave or stop his mournful howling until the trapper comes out and tries to shoot him."

He paused. This was emotional. "I've been reading quite a bit about wolf trapping and the market for their pelts. Seems the new trend of fur-lined hoods on parkas increased demand for wolf and coyote pelts. Part of the story where Isolde's fur ends up. Sad and ironic. Our screwed-up value system, eh?"

"Oh God, yes. Disgusting." She paused, thinking of the Lobo story that had got them going on this project. "I heard the same from David, my friend in the park. I asked him where do you see wolves? He said on expensive parkas in downtown Toronto!"

They both felt good about the basic elements of their story. Jonathan set to work. He had made notes on Hollie's story so he could draft a foreword about her meeting Tristan.

Hollie reviewed her photos of the Algonquin adventure on the computer. She had some great shots of the big male, and David had sent her some even better ones and he would be the model for Tristan. This made the trip worth it, she thought. She found a photo of a smaller female in the park material. She set about doing the basic drawings for the two.

Chapter Fourteen

They worked hard for over ten weeks. Jonathan would bring a new chapter and Hollie would start drawing the matching illustrations. She particularly liked doing the head shots of howling—heads flung right back, and their muzzles almost rounded at the front as if they were whistling. She also worked hard on courting behavior—especially the wolf version of holding hands. People in love cannot stop touching each other and grasp hands even when they are out and about. Same with wolves but they lean hard into each other fur on fur when they are walking and trotting along. Hollie captured this and even managed to give Tristan the big male and Isolde the smaller female looks of satisfaction. And of course, wolf kissing is licking, and she has several enthusiastic long tongue-full face licking scenes of the couple.

They wrote an endpiece that underlined Algonquin Park as the last and almost only sanctuary for the remarkable Algonquin wolf, almost the only place in North America aside from Yellowstone, where wolf packs flourished in safety. They thanked the researchers and other chroniclers of the wolf and park people who had helped and inspired them, and of course David the photographer who had been Hollie's partner in her Algonquin winter wolf adventure. They referred to the Lobo story that so moved them and that had showed them how close the wolf emotions were to their own, since both had lost beloved mates.

Finally, they were ready to bring the manuscript and illustrations to Jay Godsoe, their publisher. They both drove down to his office in a downtown tower and ceremoniously deposited the box on his desk.

He said he'd read it on the weekend. They waited nervously and drank too much Sunday night. They were both on phone extensions when it rang at ten Monday morning.

"It's quite a work. Love the illustrations. Lots of emotion in the wolf faces. But I want a different ending. Has to be hope for the pack. We're invested in its future and the sad death of Isolde, the alpha female, is a big downer to end the book on. And perhaps the male could be seen courting a new mate at the end." The writer and illustrator both let out a big breath. "Sorry, but I want this to sell, and I want a film deal. Also need a better illustration for the back cover."

"Ok," Hollie spoke up. "We can fix it. What about the title?"

"Let me think about it. *A Wolf Story* is not exactly grabby!"

"Hope you can come up with something better," Jonathan admitted.

And he did. *A Wolf Family Story* was agreed to by all. Jonathan had a great story of Tristan courting a new female Tamara, a two-year-old female from a pack in the eastern part of the park. This would end the book. It was a bit of a steal from the Theberge book in which they know a nearby collared wolf has found a mate and they sang on intermittently in unison in the still forest.

The next March a full colour oblong coffee table sized book came out with Hollie's meticulous illustration of Tristan and Isolde's profiles side by side on the cover. A dramatic illustration of Tristan in full mourning howl over the loss of Isolde replaced a pack illustration for the back cover.

There were great discussions as to where to hold the launch party. The Toronto Zoo had wolves, but they were arctic wolves. Nobody would come to Algonquin Park. The Royal Ontario Museum seemed to have one stuffed wolf in a glass case. There were wolf sculptures in a garden lawn at the entrance to the McMichael Gallery in Kleinberg north of Toronto. A possibility for sure, but too far out of the city.

In the end they decided to do it at an independent bookstore in downtown Toronto for maximum attendance. Ashleigh, stull running James PR, agreed to help. Jay was pleased and Hollie and Jonathan both did a number of radio interviews before the launch. Hollie was delighted to expand on her direct contacts with wolves in her amazing winter adventure. She always quoted the old native proverb that to look into the eyes of a wolf is to see your own soul. She had, and it had been a life-altering experience.

The invite list included all the pro-wolf advocacy group leaders and people from the park including David Robertson who came with his very lovely wife that Jonathan fussed over a bit too much, Hollie thought. John Theberge who had so inspired them was unable to come, but a couple of young wolf researchers from Trent University did. Would they find mistakes? Hollie wondered. Sammy, John and Julia came and were duly impressed, as was Christopher and his beautiful girlfriend.

It was a noisy packed affair. Hollie was asked by an art print guy whether she had considered making and selling prints of her wolf illustrations. They would talk the next week.

It seemed they had a success. Both spoke using material from the endnote almost word for word. They did not give the ending away but talked of wolf emotions and behavior and how complex and close to humans wolves were. They ended with communication and they had prearranged with David to howl, which he happily did. There was a video camera from a local station there which recorded the strange happening in the dead silent room. It was a book launch like no other.

Jay was working away at movie rights and told them there was some interest. He was insisting it had to be a live action, not an animated version. Hollie signed a deal for prints that would be advertised on an animal print site on the internet. It promised to be quite lucrative.

With the advance for the book, good orders coming in from the big bookstores and foreign rights sales going well including in the US, they decided it was time for Hollie to have a new car. In memory of Charles, she decided on a big Lexus sedan. They picked it up from the dealership the next Saturday and purred home. She felt very grand and self-indulgent.

* * * * *

Slow Love

They continued at a more leisurely pace that year. And spring brought cottage opening—a major event for the family. Both families went up in late April and the sad lonely dwelling welcomed them mutely. It was soon up and running although no running water or toilet this early. The old outhouse would have to do. Sammy and John were in charge of firing up the sauna and soon they were all crouched and sweaty and ready to jump into the very cold lake. Willow and Joe were busy chasing the chipmunk, and Hollie and Jonathan got out of the lake very quickly, dried off and went up to the cottage to start a fire.

Soon the house was cozy and drinks were served and the BBQ lit. John was in charge of the smoked pork chops and Sammy and Hollie did veggies. The easy cottage routine took hold.

"You had quite an adventure, eh? Here you went off with a big attractive photographer." Sammy wanted some gossip.

"Yes, he was a really nice guy. You saw him at the launch. Thank goodness for him. He really made sure we saw wolves. Totally platonic. We both made love calls home on his satellite phone."

"I'm not suggesting anything. Just pleased that Jonathan was so trusting with you spending days in the woods with another guy. A younger one at that."

"Well, he was sure surprised I was sixty. Felt good, and I was able to keep up with him easily."

"I bet he found you attractive."

"Perhaps. But I do work at it –but then so do you."

"In some ways you never stop being a girl!"

"True enough, for sure." Hollie reached over and hugged Sammy. Both knew exactly where the other was coming from.

Over dinner they reminisced over cottage events. The year before they had taken two canoes and paddled down the Muskoka River to Bracebridge. Christopher had brought the car to meet them above the dam and hydro installation near Highway 11. It was a very long day with several portages, and lots of laughter and some cursing as they had to walk the canoes where there were just a few inches of fast moving water. One canoe almost got away from them and Jonathan dove after it, falling into the river as he reached out for the rope. Good for a laugh then and now at the dinner table.

That night they put some oldies disks on the small CD player and both couples danced. Sammy and Hollie did a special athletic duo dance and lip sync to Cyndi Lauper's "Girls Just Want to Have Fun," and the boys clapped and cheered.

The warm feelings of cottage life overtook them all as always. They went to bed with no cares or worries.

Slow Love

Life took them back to reality and a harsh one at that the next week. Old Joe the chocolate lab stopped eating and for a day just slept and softly moaned. The vet diagnosed him with a stomach cancer and doubted he could do much. The treatment could be difficult and hugely expensive with a cancer specialist in Toronto. He was well into his teens. What were they to do? After Christopher, he was Hollie's last connection to Charles, and she loved him so much. As did Jonathan. Would they just leave him there with a local vet? They decided to take him home and see what happened.

Joe was comfortable and took a little food and stumbled out twice a day for a few days. Then he was obviously worse and back to the vets they took him, Hollie in tears. This would have to be goodbye, and she knew it. She insisted on being in the room when the vet gave him the injection. She stroked his head as he breathed his last. She cried like a child as they left the building. The wooden box with his ashes arrived a few days later and it went on the mantel in a place of honor, under her drawing of Joe Number One. Hollie hated the quiet house, not having her pal to walk in the morning and afternoon. She had a lot of photos of him on her computer and spent some time daily looking at them and wiping tears from her eyes.

But occasionally life has a way of overriding death. And that same late April Hollie was out adding bird feed to their generous feeding platform and looking down she saw a tiny sparrow on the deck below the glass sliding doors, on its back almost lifeless. It had obviously flown into the glass and was at best stunned.

She picked it up and decided she would hold it in her cupped hands, warm and comfort it and see if it revived. Jonathan emerged from his lair and took in the sight of Hollie trying to encourage the little bird, "Come on little sparrow. You'll be alright" and cooing softly. It was a very sweet moment.

Hollie kept up the recuperation attempt for a good fifteen minutes. She sat down and continued. Then Jonathan heard a cry of joy: "It's moving. I think it's going to be okay!" Hollie felt its wings trying to open and decided to take it outside. She carefully slid back the door and opened her hand. Flutter, flutter and in a few moments the tiny bird took off and flew away. She was elated. All she could think of was one living thing she was attached to had died and another had come back to life. A revealing moment which she immediately shared with Jonathan. He was obviously moved, and they embraced.

"Almost makes you believe in a greater power," he surmised.

"Sometimes I wish I did," she admitted.

They decided not to get another dog. At least for the moment. Neither wanted to have to go through the loss again. They had met an older woman in the woods a while back who did not have a dog and said her reason for not getting another was that. The pain of loss was too great to want to experience again. They both understood now what she meant. And that's what they told family and friends who were so accustomed to them having a canine member of the family.

They decided that the death of a beloved pet was a subject for a kid's book since many kids have that experience, particularly dogs who were killed by cars. Hollie remembered Charles telling of the road death of Peter, their beloved cocker spaniel when he was six and the impression it had made on him.

They ran it by Jay, and he liked it if it ended on a positive note. They agonized over that. Would a ceremonial burying of the deceased help kids get over it? No sense pretending the pet had gone to heaven—not in this post-Christian era. On the other hand, Indigenous peoples believe all living things have souls. However, Hollie did a little research on the afterlife in native cultures. No mention of it being shared by dogs, who had been sometimes ritually eaten. So, they were left with the more normal fix for kids, the fairly quick one of getting another dog. So it would be.

The book would be set on a farm with two kids a boy and a girl, Sally aged seven and Don aged nine. The dog would be a lively border collie named Dollie. It would be for kids six-to-nine. There would be several adventures with the kids and the dog, and Dollie would be heroic in at least one.

While Jonathan was sketching out the story, the adventures and Dollie's heroism when Sally fell through the ice in a pond, and the devotion of Sally to the dog who slept with her, Hollie was drawing the characters and the dog. But she was also ruminating on the key moment in the story, that was how did the mother comfort her bereaved daughter?

She even dreamt about a dialogue that would convey a guiding principle in her life—that love never dies. She talked about this idea to Jonathan who came up with a bedside conversation that would end the book. He knew how important the principle was to Hollie and tried to capture it.

This was what he came up with:

> Nancy heard her daughter sobbing in her room the night after Dollie had been killed running across the highway after a squirrel.
>
> Nancy entered the room quietly and sat on the edge of the bed and took her daughter's hand.

"It's really tough losing a good friend, isn't it?" Sally wiped her tears and started sniffling and hugged her mom.

"It is really horrible. I can't believe she's gone. I can still see her at the bottom of my bed. I'll never stop missing her…"

"I had a dog that slept on my bed when I was growing up. He died when I was ten, and I never stopped missing her. But you know what my mom told me?"

"What?"

"That love never dies. Didn't Dollie love you very very much? And you loved her so much, too."

"Yes, for sure—remember she saved me from drowning? She was my best friend. I told her all my secrets and she understood, I know."

"Well, that love doesn't stop just because she's not here. It continues, and you carry it in your heart and think about it, and it makes you feel better, because it's still real. And her love for you is the same. It stays and will still make you feel good and happy."

"Do you really believe that?"

> "Yes, I do, and it will take away the worst sadness. I know. You have a good imagination, think of her still at the end of the bed."
>
> "I will. Thanks mom." Sally grabbed her pillow and hugged it.

"I love it. It's a better ending than them getting a new dog." Hollie was moved and thought of how she had dealt with the loss of Charles. She truly believed that love never died, and it worked for a child and the loss of a pet. It had also been the motivating power for the wolf story too. It was what her life was all about.

The Author

Patrick Gossage

Patrick is a veteran commentator, writer, public relations professional, political operative and community activist.

He was the press secretary to Prime Minister Pierre Trudeau in the late seventies and early eighties and chronicled these years in a book based on his diaries, *Close to the Charisma* (1986, McClelland and Stewart). He founded a successful PR agency in Toronto and is now retired in the suburbs with his wife Helga and dog Annie. Walking her in a neighborhood woodlot with a wonderful group of dog lovers was the initial inspiration for this book.